Persuasive Contracts

By: TyeMease

Chapter 1

"Go get the car Gordo."

"Alright," Gordo responded knowing his duties.

Within five minutes he was out front beeping the horn for Antonio to come out. He posted up outside of the driver side door making sure everything was clear. Antonio had a lot of beef, so Gordo had to be on point, because Antonio wasn't. He came stumbling out of the bar. He had way too much to drink.

"Where to boss?"

"I don't know, take me somewhere, anywhere, the night is still young."

Gordo was Antonio's driver and flunky. He did anything without asking any questions. They had just came out of the bar that Antonio's friend Nudo owned on River Road in the Camerhill section of Camden.

"Anywhere huh," Gordo asked a little excited? To him that meant he was able to choose for once. "Would you like to go to this whore house? All Morena's (black women). Their all pretty boss, I'm telling you, I always go there."

Gordo was a trick and wasn't ashamed of it. That's how he got majority of his pussy.

"Let's go," Antonio said in his play voice. He took the Black and Mild out of the ashtray and lit it. He inhaled deep, then leaned back in his seat. To him wasn't nothing like a Black and Mild when he was drunk. He wouldn't even champ them all the way, because he would be in such a rush to smoke.

Antonio was the head of the Latin Kings in Camden, a position he held for the last three years. It seemed like only yesterday he got crowned king. After years of putting in work, he finally got called to the round table. Antonio's named had came up on the list, bypassing other older eligible guys that felt as though they should have been next up. His crowning rubbed a lot of guys with money and power the wrong way, it caused malice toward him.

Antonio was chosen for many reasons. He was smart, he put in work, got money, and for the most part knew how to move. Being only twenty-nine made him the youngest leader within the Latin King organization. Over the years Antonio had made a lot of enemies. He had killed or gotten killed a lot of dudes. Mainly other kings over money, drugs, or just disobeying an order out of hate.

They pulled up on Sheridan Street and got out. Gordo knocked on the door. After a few knocks this beautiful light skin woman answered the door. She had to be about 5'7, but the six inch heels she wore made her look much taller. She had legs like Beyonce. Her skirt was so short that her thighs were basically showing. With no bra on her breast sat up and her nipples made themselves known. Her face resembled that of the actress Lisa Ray. Antonio was struck by her beauty. Being drunk, he wasn't aware that he was stuck in awe. He couldn't figure out how someone so beautiful could be a whore when she could easily have a man taking care of her.

"Hey Gordo," Keisha said letting them in. "Who's your friend?"

Keisha kept smiling at how Antonio was checking her out. He was too drunk to be aware of his facial expressions. Once she let them in, she began walking in front of them, each cheek marching left right left right. Her skirt raising little by little trying to reveal the bottom of her butt. She didn't bother to pull it down. She gave them everything they wanted to see.

"This is Antonio, the boss, so bring out your best."

Usually while there Gordo acted like a shy little boy, but today he had his chest out and his grown man voice on.

"You know all we have are fly honeys here," Kiesha said.

"Dam, her ass fat as hell," Antonio whispered to Gordo.

Kiesha heard him, but acted like she didn't. She knew she had a stuffy. Like every dude that came there they was on it, that's why she let her skirt rise. Kiesha was the Madam of the Black Barbie House. It was well known in South Jersey. Most of the women there were women from Camden or women who came to Camden at one time, got turned out and never left. Their main clientele consisted of dudes from the outskirts, working guys and young hustlers that was more than willing to pay for some pussy.

Kiesha rung a bell that was on the table and seven girls came walking down the stairs like they were trying out for Miss America. All of them beautiful, thick with no stomachs. They were looking like stallions as they stood in line in their six inch heels in front of Antonio and Gordo.

Kiesha had them turn around to display their assets. Gordo was waiting for Antonio to pick who he wanted so he could pick his regular. All the ladies were

6

staring at Antonio like they wanted him to pick them, even Gordo's regular. Gordo was praying that his boss didn't pick her though. On the low he had feelings for her. Antonio already had his mind set on who he wanted from the moment she opened the door.

"They're all pretty but I want you," Antonio said undressing Kiesha with his eyes.

She started blushing, she kind of seen it coming.

"Sorry I'm the boss, so I'm off limits, but these pretty ladies will take care of all your needs."

Kiesha had started off in this game early, at the age of fourteen. Now at thirty two she was trying not to be active and use the new girls that didn't know anything about the game the same way the pimps used to use her to make money.

"I got five hundred for you," Antonio said.

Kiesha couldn't refuse that if she wanted to, especially not in front of the girls. She was teaching them to get that paper. She had to lead by example. Yet she knew if he was willing to come up five hundred then he was willing to come up a stack.

"Hold up, we'll talk. Go ahead Gordo, pick."

As usual Gordo picked his favorite girl Tee Tee. All the rest of the ladies went back to doing what they were doing.

"So, what's up," Antonio asked pushing up on Kiesha?"

"Give me a thousand," she said trying her hand. She knew that if a man really wanted it that he wouldn't hold any expenses.

"Dam you going to charge me a stack? That better be the best pussy ever."

"I been told something like that before, but you can give me ya opinion after I throw it on you."

She led Antonio down the basement so they could be alone. Down there was a couch and a t.v.. Under the front porch area was a room with a bed in it. That's where they ended up.

"Purse first," Kiesha said with her hand out.

She learned from the pimps she used to ho for to always get the money first.

"I can't believe you really going to charge me a stack to fuck. If ma dick wasn't hard from the moment I saw you I wouldn't be coming out ma pocket like this," Antonio said pulling a wad of hundreds out of his pocket. A thousand dollars was chump change to him.

Still, he didn't think he'll ever pay that much for some pussy, he was used to women throwing themselves at him.

Once she got the money, she put it away and gave him a condom. They both came out of their clothes. He put the condom on, then bent her over the bed. He started going hard from the door. He was drunk and in his mind, he was going to get his thousand dollars worth. She moaned as their bodies hit, making clapping noises. Her ass jingled every time he rammed her. He grabbed her by the neck and mushed her head down on the covers while he drilled her.

"Turn over bitch, a thousand dollars huh? Fuck is wrong with you." Antonio was sweating profusely. He was acting mad at the pussy. He put her in the missionary position and began beating it up like he was trying to break her pelvis. He hit it for another half an hour, then she started sucking him off. After his second nut, he was finished, too drunk to continue. He wasn't sure if her shot was worth a thousand dollars, but he knew that he'll be back. "I could get used to this. I promise I won't be so rough next time."

The next day Antonio came back, and the day after that. They were hooking up on the regular, eventually she stopped charging him, but he would still give her money. What started out as business ended up being pleasure for the both of them. He couldn't help but want to possess her. Over the months he had been trying to talk her out of her profession. He wanted to take care of her, but she wasn't trying to hear it. She didn't want to depend on a man. She had been under the thumb of many pimps before and because of the things she went through she told herself that she wouldn't be under a man ever again. She wasn't opposed to the friendship her and Antonio had, as long as he treated her good. He definitely treated her good in the beginning, but he had anger problems. The more they got attached to each other, the more he began flipping when he didn't get his way.

Kiesha had opened the door to let Antonio in. They went upstairs to her room.

"What's so important that I had to stop what I was doing."

"I'm pregnant."

"Yeah, is it mine?"

"It's yours Antonio, I'm sure of that."

No matter how sure she was she still was a whore, so he knew to get a DNA test. If it was his this would be his first child. He had been messing with his lady for years now and she have yet to give him a child.

"So, what are you going to do," Antonio asked?

"I want to keep it…."

"I want you to keep it too," he said cutting her off. "I'll get you a nice house on the outskirts and take care of you and the baby. Fuck this shit right here," he said referring to the house. Money ain't nothing, you ain't never going to have to worry about that again.

Keisha sat quiet listening to him. She could tell that he really wanted her to have the baby, but he also wanted her to give her lifestyle up. That was going to be a problem for her. Unlike many females she knew, she wasn't looking for a free ride from a man with money because she knew the conditions that came with it. Instead of spoiling the plans he was making for her without her permission, she just let him ramble.

After that day she went back to business as usual. After a while, when he seen she wasn't making plans to leave the Black Barbie House they started having arguments and he became abusive, mentally and physically, but he couldn't beat her ass how he wanted because he didn't want her to lose the baby. He told her that no child of his was going to grow up in a whore house. Over the months Keisha's stomach got bigger and bigger. Antonio wasn't going over there how he used to and when he did, he would be drunk on some bullshit, trying to house the pussy.

One day when Keisha was seven months pregnant Antonio showed up at the Black Barbie House. She didn't want to let him in, but she did anyway. He came in kissing and feeling on her, but she wasn't beat. Every time he tried to kiss her, she would turn the other way. Then he grabbed her by her face squeezing her jaws. Her face looked like she was making a fish face.

"Bitch, stop turning away from me," he demanded.

Then he kissed her and licked her face. He grabbed her by her hair and pulled her down the basement. He was too strong for her, so she never fought back, plus she didn't want to risk losing her baby. At this point she hated him, and he hated her, but at the same time he loved her. He hated her because she wouldn't do what he wanted like everyone else did. That's why he treated her like shit.

Keisha had on one of them dresses that pregnant women wore. He pulled her panties down, making her take one leg out of them. He bent her over and kicked her legs apart how the police do dudes when they are about to search them. She couldn't bend all the way over because of her stomach so she had to brace herself on the wall. He lifted her dress up and began hitting her in the butt, ravishing her with no mercy. Keisha grunted and cried the whole time.

A couple months later Keisha gave birth to a healthy baby boy. She named him Royal McKennie. Beings as though she didn't have any family the baby stayed with her at the Black Barbie House, under the supervision of herself and the other girls. They all adored him and treated him like their own.

Antonio would come sometimes to play with his son. That visit always ended with them arguing. Fed up Antonio showed up at the house with two of his men. When they went in Tee Tee was holding the baby. She gave him the baby when he asked. When Keisha came downstairs, he was playing with the baby. He told her to go get some clothes and pampers. She asked where they were going, and he told her to go see his family.

****

"Who baby is this," Antonio's mother asked as he gave Roy to her to hold?

"Mines mom," he said with a smile. "I need for him to stay here for a while. I'm about to go home."

"Where's his mother at?" His mom didn't know that he had a baby. She never met Keisha. "I hope you didn't kidnap this child. I'm too old to be going to jail."

"Nah mom, you good."

His mother sensed something wasn't right. She knew her son was crazy.

Antonio never took Roy back to the Black Barbie House. Hoping that Keisha would stop dealing with it, he told her that she wasn't getting the baby back until she did. That didn't work, she chose to continue on with her life. Because of the people and things she surrounded herself with, she felt as though the baby would be better off with his family. The grandmom got stuck with the baby. It eventually got to the point when they met and Keisha was able to see her baby.

Chapter 2

"What's up with June, did you talk to him?"

"Yeah, I talk to him, but he act like he aint doing nothing."

"What he say," Antonio asked?

"He aint doing nothing," Ricco responded.

"Fuck it, kill em then and whoever else out there who want to be stupid. They're going to know that I aint to be fucked with."

Antonio was trying to take over the dope set on 26th and Federal, but June wasn't folding to the pressure. Ricco was tired of how Antonio was barking orders. He kept him on these senseless missions. He felt like his money wasn't adding up to the work he was putting in. Antonio was the kind of leader that was respected because he was feared, even by his own men.

Ricco walked in Lee's breakfast spot on federal street. June was already in there waiting. Ricco walked pass the old Chinese dude standing there looking like Mr. Miyagi and took a seat at the table in front of June.

"What's up, what could this be about, because if it's the same thing you already know my answer."

"He want me to get at you, but you ma dude. We grew up together. I'm on it like fuck this dude because he on some other type time."

"So, what you saying," June asked?

"I'm talking about flipping the script. Murdering him, then I come get money with you."

"Alright, what you need me for then?"

"He wanted me to body you. You don't want to get at him for that? If I wouldn't have came to you he would of made it happen."

Ricco and June talked for a while longer. At the end of their discussion June told Ricco to handle it, and then come see him. June wasn't sure if he was trying to set him up or what.

****

Ricco and Rampage sat in a car across the street from Antonio's house. They seen the kitchen light flickering on and off. That was Lexus giving them the signal they had been waiting for. Lexus was Antonio's girl, but Ricco had been smashing on the low. Really after she had found out that Antonio had a baby on her. She had ran into Ricco's arms and him being the slimball he was took advantage of the situation. The plan was once Antonio was in the bed Lexus would open the door for Ricco.

They got out of the car and went through the back door. Lexus was still in the kitchen, they walked right pass her without saying anything and went upstairs. Rampage was the lead man. When he opened the room door he didn't see anybody in the bed or in the room.

"He's not in here," he whispered.

Ricco stuck his head in the room for a look. They started tip toeing back down the hall to see where he was at.

Antonio had just got done taking a piss when he seen them creep by. He was in the bathroom without his gun or anything else that he could use to protect himself. He heard them coming back down the hall checking rooms. When Rampage got to the bathroom Antonio pounced on him, trying to get the gun out of his hand. While they were tussling Antonio seen Ricco trying to get a good shot. The thought of his supposed to be manz crossing him made him fight even harder. He got extra strong on Rampage and started manhandling him, but Rampage didn't let that gun go.

Antonio tried to keep Rampage between him and Ricco. He couldn't believe Ricco was trying to kill him. After all they been through together. After everything he did for Ricco. They had the gun in the air. All Rampage was worried about was not letting that thing go.

"Bang"

The gun went off. By then Ricco had gotten close enough to shoot Antonio in the shoulder. Antonio let go of the gun and grabbed his shoulder. Rampage stepped back and Ricco started letting lose on Antonio. They shot him twenty three times. When they turned to run down the steps a seven year old boy was standing in the doorway of his room. Awaken from the noise of them tussling he got up in time to witness the murder of his father.

Rampage and Roy made eye contact for a split second. Not trying to leave any witnesses Rampage put the burner to Roy's head. "Nah, come on. He's just a kid," Ricco said pulling Rampage. To Rampage it didn't matter. He had two eyes and a pair of lips, that meant he was able to tell. He hesitated, but then left without harming Roy.

Lexus was still in the kitchen standing near the door. She opened it for them when she saw them coming. Before Rampage left, he put the burner to Lexus head and blew her top off before Ricco could object to anything. Ricco didn't have plans on killing her, but Rampage did. He didn't trust anyone enough to give them that pass. He didn't like that the little boy had seen his face.

****

The next day at one of June's cribs on 25th street Ricco was there trying to get their business relationship off on a good foot. He had got surprised when during their conversation June's manz had put the burner to him.

"What's this June? I thought we was going to make something happen."

Ricco sat in a chair while six dudes surrounded him.

"I can't trust you, you just crossed ya manz. I know you'll cross me. I thank you for handling that for me though."

"Come on June, don't do this, I'll do anything you want."

Ricco was in the middle of begging for his life when one of June's men put a plastic bag over his head and started suffocating him. The other dudes held him down. He tried kicking and struggling for about a minute, but then he stopped moving.

Chapter 3

Twelve Years Later

"Dedra got a friend, you trying to shoot over there with me?"

"What she look like," Roy asked?

"I don't know but pussy don't got no face. Plus, you aint trying to make her ya girl."

"You right, I'm with it. Dedra don't really be with no bum chicks anyway."

"All of a sudden you got standards, you kills me."

Roy pulled up to the house on Lansdowne. When they went in Tone went straight upstairs. Roy sat on the couch and started talking to Aunt Rosa. He had became like family. Tone's dad and uncles were all drug dealers. They owned the store on the Camelot (Louis and Lansdowne). The Camelot was a drug set. Tone's family was Dominicans, so they easily fitted in with everyone in the neighborhood. Not only that, but they were also connects.

19

When Tone came back downstairs, they left the house. Before they could pull off Fernando came up to the car. He had on some tailor made slacks, a silk shirt and some gaiters shoes with a bunch of jewelry on. He looked like he was going to an 80's night club in Miami. That was him every day though. He had a book bag in his hand when he walked up to the passenger side door. Tone rolled down the window to see what he wanted.

"I need a favor from ya'll."

"What's that," Tone asked?

"I need you to drop this bookbag off at 45th street Pub for me."

"How much," Roy asked?

"What you mean how much," Fernando asked looking at Roy like he was out of pocket for asking that?

"I'm saying, I'm driving and if I'm going to risk ma freedom the price has to be right," Roy responded not backing down.

Fernando stared at him with the stone face. If he had any idea that Roy was some nut young boy it was gone, but he still had to test him.

"You don't even know what's in it."

"Hold up, don't tell me, coke right," Roy responded being sarcastic?

Fernando let out a little laugh. "Alright smart ass, how much you want?"

Tone looked at Roy waiting for him to spit it out. He found it funny how Roy was trying to game his uncle and it seem to have been working. Even though Tone grew up around all hustlers, they always told him to go to school and kept him away from what they were into. Even though hanging with Roy he was into a lot of things. They smoked, drank, partied, and chased chicks. Everything but sold drugs.

"A stack a piece," he said trying to hold a serious face.

"What! Come on now, ya'll only going out east. I'll give ya'll five hundred a piece."

"Alright," Roy agreed.

"I got ya'll when ya'll get back," Fernando said putting the bookbag on Tone's lap. "Give it to the tall dark skinny dude playing pool. His name Fah."

"Is he going to give us something for it," Roy asked?

"Nah, that's taken care of."

Roy pulled off heading for his destination.

"Five hundred, you got that off," Tone said excited.

"Got what off? That's business, aint nothing in the world free. Every real businessman knows that. I definitely wasn't going to risk my freedom for nothing."

Tone looked in the book bag. It was four bricks in there. He turned it towards Roy so he could see.

"I knew it," was all that Roy said.

When they got to the Pub Roy put the bookbag on. Once inside he walked over to where Fah was. Him and his guys were shooting pool. Tone had went to order some food. When he came back Roy was talking trash to Fah about taking his money in pool. Roy loved to gamble.

They could have went in there and dropped the bookbag off, but it wouldn't of taken a rocket scientist to figure out what just happened. Even though they weren't in the game yet, they knew how things went. Bout time Fah beat Roy in a game of pool the food was ready. Roy laughed it off and took his loss like a good sport. Afterwards him and Tone sat down and ate.

****

"What took ya'll so long," Fernando asked as they walked through the door?

"We had to chill for a little. We didn't just want to drop it off and leave. That would have been too obvious."

Fernando already had the money waiting. He dug in his pocket and gave it to them.

"Nice doing business with ya'll."

"Nice doing business with you," Roy said counting his money. "I hope we could do this more often."

"What you know about the coke business," Fernando asked Roy?

Roy didn't know much, but his father had been a big time drug dealer and that a couple of his manz was going hand to hand trapping on blocks.

"I know a little something. Ma dad used to be heavy in the game."

"Who ya pops?"

"Antonio, He dead now though."

"Antonio Antonio," Fernando said digging in his memory bank. "I think I remember ya pops. He was Latin King, right?

"Yeah," Roy happily responded.

"I remember him and his manz Ricco. Yeah man, whenever you want to make some money come through, I'll keep you busy. There is one rule you must live and die by though, no snitching," Fernando said not even giving him a chance to respond. He wanted to tell him, so it'll be clear.

"That was the first thing my pop taught me."

"Good, he was a good father then."

When Fernando told Roy to come through when he wanted to make some money, he didn't know that Roy was going to be there every day. Over the next couple of months Roy made moves for Fernando, sometimes without Tone. He worked his way into Fernando's circle and soaked up all the game he could. Fernando was well connected. All the dudes around him were old head Dominican dudes who got money on the low.

Roy began handling all the local weight sales. He was getting real fly with all the dudes he was serving and they respected him. He eventually opened a weed set on Atlantic, but more so in the alley. They sold a few different strains on that block, but he also had built up his clientele with dudes who he came up with that sold coke. He was trying to get it from every angle.

Friday night D's place was packed. People from all over was there. Roy, Tone and Shon went there together. They didn't like to roll deep. They knew that brought unwanted attention and drama. Roy wasn't with that. He was about money.

While Roy was playing the wall when this thick chick came backing it up on him. He wasn't really the dancing type, so he just grinned on her. Roy was about 5'9 and skinny. O girl he was dancing with was extra thick and was throwing it on him. It kind of looked like he was trying to ride a bull.

"You know you can't dance," Garnett told Roy.

"O shit, what's good my guy?"

"Let me holla at you bro."

"Alright, hold up," Roy said. "You leaving with me," he asked the chick he was dancing with?

She nodded her head yeah and he went to go talk to Garnett.

"What them things going for," Garnett asked referring to the coke prices?

"32,000 right now. Whenever you ready come through."

"Alright, I might come see you tomorrow."

"Alright, they on deck so whenever, I got you."

They shook hands before Garnett went about his business. Roy knew Garnett for years. His squad got a lot of money, but they also did a lot of dirt as well. Roy had that lingering in the back of his mind. That wasn't going to stop him from dealing with Garnett. A lot of dudes he sold weight to did dirt. They were all gangstas living the same lifestyle. There were times when he heard that this person killed such and such and the next day that person was buying coke off of him. He wasn't worried about people personal lives, he was about his business. It's hard to survive in a pool for of sharks if you're scared.

Fifteen minutes later some chaos broke out on the other side of the club. Roy and his guys got out of there with a few ladies.

Some dude tried to snatch Game's chain. He pulled on it with all his might, but it didn't pop. Game started punishing dude. Dude manz tried to shoot him some bail. Garnett seen him and put him down with a right hook. Dude slid across the floor. Another one of their men stole Garnett, but it aint faze him. He looked at him like he was stupid and began walking towards him. Dudes had the fear of God in his eyes as he backed up. J.B. came from the back of dude and monkey dunked him on his neck. It was two more dudes that was with them that they ended beating up.

The fight spilled outside. Garnett and his dudes were deep. They were recking out. When the cops came they were dispersing. Garnett got in his car and pulled off. As soon as they got on the highway the cops pulled them over.

"Dam, I knew they were going to pull us. Ya'll got anything on ya'll?"

"I got a couple bags of haze on me," JB said.

"I got ma strap on me," Garnett said.

"Pull off on them," Game said.

"That's the plan."

Garnett pulled over, put the car in neutral and took his foot off of the brakes so the brake lights wouldn't be on. There was a little space in between the cars. Two cops got out. They were walking on each side of the car. As soon as they got close enough Garnett released the emergency brake, put the car in drive and floored it. The ass of the impala dropped as it took off.

The two out of shape cops ran back to their squad car. Bout time they got to it Garnett was more than a block away. They still took chase. D's place wasn't far from Camden. They made it back with a chain of sirens behind them. Garnett got to Whitman and Louis and slammed on the breaks. They all got out of the car running. One cop tried to run them down, but they all hit different alleyways. Another cop had to stop the car from rolling. The police surrounded the area, but no one was caught.

****

Monday morning Garnett was up. He was one of them people who didn't need much sleep. He was always on go. He got up and went in the bathroom. Fee was in the mirror when he came in there and started taking a piss. He was taking one of them long pisses, but what irritated fee was that he didn't bother to lift the toilet seat up before doing so. She always told him about that, yet she would end up sitting on a wet toilet seat.

"I guess you forgot to lift the seat up again, huh?"

"I had to go bad, I aint have time for that."

"Make sure you clean that up with some disaffect Fee said with an attitude."

"Alright, it's too early for you to be starting."

Fee just shook her head and kept doing her hair. After he got done cleaning up, he washed his hands. She moved over a bit for him to do so. They were both looking in the mirror when he asked her, "You still love me."

She sucked her teeth, "you're ignorant, you don't think of nobody but yourself."

"I'm sorry," he said grinding on her butt.

She had this red panty and bra set on and he had on his boxers. Fee was caramel complexion, short and thick in all the right places. Her butt was more wide than plumped though. Garnett began kissing on her neck.

"I'ma remember next time. You love me," he asked again while laying little kisses on her neck? He reached into the front of her panties and started playing with her click. Already wet from the kisses and him grinding on her butt, she stopped doing her hair. Now she was moaning and rolling her hips. After she came, he pulled her panties down, bent her over the sink and started hitting it.

"Oh Garnett, don't wake the baby."

The bathroom door was open, but he kept hitting it harder and faster trying to get his nut.

"You love me, don't you," he said pulling her hair?

"Yes yes, oh oh." Now she was loud enough to wake the baby.

"Yes what?"

"Yes, I love you, I love you, I love you oh oh."

"You don't love me, you love this dick."

He kept talking to her and she was loving it. They both came and stayed there stuck like two dogs. After about thirty seconds of resting in it, he got up and the juices that flowed between them came out like slime.

"Stop saying that too."

"What?"

"That I don't love you, I only love ya dick."

"You know I'm liable to say anything while we getting it in. I aint mean it," he said and smacked her on the butt making that thing jiggle.

Garnett turned around and seen his daughter Kalia standing in the doorway with her pacifier in her mouth.

"See, you woke the baby up," Garnett said.

....

Garnett didn't get a chance to get up with Roy like he wanted to. Too many things had came up, and he kind of pushed it to the back of his mind.

Riding through SB (Carl Miller Blvd) he spotted General. He pretended not to see him. Him and his dudes had been talking about moving in on General and taking his block. General had an all weed flow that did numbers. Garnett pulled up on 8th street, got out and went into one of the apartments. Duke seen him and followed him in there.

"Yo, put that Jezzy on," Garnett told Duke.

Garnett wanted to hear some get money music while he cooked up. Once he was done cheffing the coke he gave Duke a half of brick to bag up, then he tucked the other half. They got outside and walked around the building and got swarmed by cops from every angle. It was nowhere for them to run. They both put there hands up. All Garnett could think about was how much time he had left on parole.

The police handcuffed and searched them. They found a gun and eighteen ounces on Duke, and a gun and twenty three ounces on Garnett.

"Look what we have here. Y'all fell right into our arms," one of the cops said.

"He's not even the guy we're looking for," one of the other officers said referring to Duke. They were looking for some dudes who had escaped from Lakeland Youth Correctional Facility. They got a call that they were in the area and Duke resembled one of them.

Chapter 4

Knock knock knock knock.

"Who the hell is that," Roy said to himself. It sounded like the police. He hid his burner in a stash spot in the couch. "Daniel," he hollered. "Come get the door."

Daniel came downstairs and looked through the peep hole, then opened the door."

"It's Shon," she said given him a certain look thinking, *you scary mothafucka.*

"Why you knocking like you the police?"

"Ma bad bro, you got that light ass door," Shon said walking in the house. "You in here watching the animal channel?"

"This that work. You don't know nothing about it. Look, watch how this Tiger run down on that Zebra. Got em, told you. I told you," Roy said excited like he was watching a football game or something.

"You really off this shit, huh?"

"Hell yeah, what you watch Jerry Springer when you in the crib," Roy said being sarcastic.

"Nah, BET and MTV. Everything I wonna see is on those two channels."

"I bet it is."

"Here go that money. It's banging like a dope flow out there," Shon said referring to the weed flow on Atlantic. "You might as well put some coke out there. Fiends stay coming through asking do we have any."

"I just might. I been thinking about opening a coke block."

"I'm out of here, I just came to give you that. What you doing later?"

"I gotta get up with Fernando."

****

Roy went into the store on the Camelot. Tone's other aunt Luci was behind the counter.

"How you doing Ms. Luci," Roy said as he walked pass her? He knocked on the back door and Fernando answered and let him in. Fernando was smoking a cigar, he went straight to the mini bar and poured himself something to drink.

"You want something to drink?"

"Sure, I'll take something."

Fernando brought Roy some of what he was drinking and handed him a cigar. Roy wasn't a cigar smoker, but he knew you didn't have to inhale it, so when Fernando lit his cigar for him, he took a couple of pulls to taste it. With the cognac in one hand and a cigar in the other, Roy felt like a boss.

"I'm going to New York for a couple of days, I need you to take care of things while I'm gone." He scooted the mini bar over about three feet, lifted the carpet then pulled out ten bricks of coke. "These should last you until I get back. Put them in that bag over there and on ya way out put some loaves of bread or something on top so it could look like you bought something."

Roy left and went to his grand mom house. Grandmom was in the kitchen cooking up a storm.

"What's for dinner," Roy asked as he gave his grandmom a kiss on the cheek?

"We're having your favorite, are you eating with us today?"

"Yup, I aint going nowhere."

Roy went back outside and got the bag out of his car and put it in the other car he used for a stash spot. He kept that car a couple houses down from his grandmom's. He drove it every so often, but that was just so people wouldn't get it towed. It was mainly a stash spot. He took the bread out of the bag and into the house.

"Have you seen your mother?"

"No mama, why?"

"She was over here the other day. She seems happy. You know she got a new man, right?"

"I aint know that. I wonder how long that's going to last."

Roy and his mother Keisha didn't have the best mother and son relationship when he was growing up, but she always used to stop by and show him love and bring him toys, like water guns and as he got older bikes and stuff like that. They were always cordial, and he loved her.

Later that night Roy was in front of Niyumi's on Atlantic getting some chips and things when he seen Rasheed riding down Norris. He flagged him over.

"Dam fam, it's like you just vanished from the face of the earth."

"Nah bro, I was coming through to let you know I need another week or two," Rasheed lied. He had been ducking Roy and was cursing himself for riding down that block.

"How long do it take to move a brick, what you took a loss?"

"Nah, shit just slow," Rasheed said in his slow deep baritone voice.

Rasheed got money on the Camelot which was one of the known sets in Camden for crack cocaine. Roy always went around that area to Fernando's store, so he knew it wasn't slow. He felt like Rasheed was trying to play him out. Not only because it's been two in a half weeks since he fronted him the brick, but because of Rasheed's attitude. He had one of them tough man attitudes and he made it seem like he wasn't in a rush to get Roy his money.

Roy was about 5'9 and skinny. He was getting money and has yet to put in any work, so it was only a matter of time before somebody tested him. Roy was definitely feeling like he was being tested. He could see it in Rasheed's eyes that he didn't have any attentions on paying him.

"By next Friday I should have everything for you," Rasheed said.

Roy had let him go, but he thought about it, today was Friday. Now he definitely knew Rasheed on was on some BS.

CHAPTER 5

Fernando visited a couple family members when he first arrived in the city. New York was like his second home. Growing up he spent a lot of time going back and forth from Camden to New York which was where his father was from. All the dudes in his family were known for getting money. They were rich. A couple were dead and in prison, but the ones that was home was doing it.

Fernando had a diner meeting with his uncle Tuco. Afterwards he went to the hotel he was staying at. He got on the elevator and pressed five for the fifth floor. Before the door could shut three dudes ran in there on him. Instinctively he jumped back when he seen the knife in the first dude hand. He tussled with him for the knife while the other two dudes were trying to stab him. He finally got the knife from dude and started stabbing too. When the elevator door opened two dudes ran out. One of them noticed that their manz wasn't with them so he doubled back and tried picking his manz up. Dude got up, took a few steps, then fell. His manz tried helping him again, but when he wasn't getting up, he left. The other dude had been left. Fernando was on the elevator floor. They stabbed him up pretty bad. When he got to the hospital he was in critical condition. He had gotten stabbed nine times, luckily he survived. He had got locked up because one of the guys he stabbed died.

****

"Hello," Roy answered his phone.

"Where you at," Tone asked?

"I just turned on Atlantic, why?"

"I'll tell you."

Roy pulled up and Tone jumped in the car with him.

"Head to the store. Fernando got locked up in New York for a body. They stabbed him up and he killed one of them."

"Who?"

"I don't know, they be going through their own beefs up there."

When Roy pulled up to the Camelot he seen a bunch of dudes on Lansdowne. He spotted Rasheed. That Friday he was supposed to pay Roy had came and went. Rasheed never looked that way. Roy wasn't sure if he seen him or not but at the moment he had other things to worry about.

When Roy left the store, he seen Rasheed outside talking, moving his arms like he was some sort of rapper. *He over there entertaining,* Roy thought to himself. He seen his chain swinging and wrist icy. Roy knew that he was being tested. He knew if he let this ride then dudes a try to play em like he was sweet. As he rode by Rasheed looked at the car nonchalantly and kept on talking.

Roy was already upset because of Fernando's situation, now Rasheed had him furious. *I gotta show this pussy that he fucking with the wrong one.* Roy didn't waste any time. He called his manz Jeff whom he be serving. Jeff was a wild boy, Roy knew that he'll be with whatever. Jeff pulled up on Atlantic with two other dudes.

"I need you to put some work in for me."

"Anything for you bro. Just point me in the right direction."

"You know Rasheed from the Camelot?"

"Nah, I can find out who he is though."

"I know who he is already, he owe me money. He around there right now. I want you to get at him for me. I got ten stacks for you."

"Ten stacks, what you want me to kill his mom too because you know I would have done it for you for free, but I can use that for something."

Roy always looked Jeff out, so he was more than willing to put some work in for him. Jeff got in the car and rode around to the Camelot. One of Jeff's manz knew who Rasheed was, but didn't know him personally. He let Jeff know who he was as they pulled up.

"Who Rasheed," Jeff asked as his manz pulled up on the crowd of dudes who was out there talking? It was less of them out there than when Ray saw them.

"Why, who wonna know," Rasheed asked?

"I got something for you."

"He aint around here right now, but I'll tell him y'all came through," Rasheed said suspicious of their motives. What he didn't know was that they already knew who he was.

"Just give him this for me," Jeff said. He pointed the burner out the window at Rasheed and let loose hitting him in the stomach and chest. Jeff and his dudes pulled off like it was nothing.

****

"1 through 15 mess out," the C.O. yelled loud enough to wake Garnett out of his street dreams. That's the only time he knew he'll be seeing them for at least another nine months when he finished his parole violation and could make bail on them other charges.

Garnett got up, washed his face, brushed his teeth and waited for them to call his room number. Sunday was visit day, and Fee was to make her usual afternoon visit. When they called rec out Garnett went outside and started working out with his workout squad. His workout squad consisted of two Newark dudes and one dude from Penns Grove. He only dealt with Camden dudes that he knew or had gotten to know and who was thorough. Over the years they had stop making Camden dudes how they used to, so he had to watch his company. Real recognize real no matter where dudes were at or from. After the workout Garnett went back, took a shower, freshened up and laid down and dozed off.

A few hours later Garnett walked in the visit hall and spotted Fee. He went to the C.O. desk to sign in then he went over to Fee and gave her a big hug and a passionate kiss. All while squeezing her ass.

"Dam, you got ma pussy wet," Fee said as they sat down.

They sat opposite of one another. That was prison policy. Southwoods State Prison was one of the biggest and whackest prisons in New Jersey.

"You aint gotta bring this up no more, I got another way. Game is going to bring something by and somebody else is going to come get it, alright?"

"Ok," Fee said. She was happy she didn't have to risk her freedom anymore. Even though she was willing to do anything Garnett had told her to do. Garnett took a drink of his bottled water. Fee kept kissing and touching on him. A c.o. lady came over to them and told them that they were too close, that they had to back up a bit. Afterwards she wobbled back over to where she was standing so she could watch the visits for any suspicious activity.

"She hating because she busted," Fee said.

Garnett started laughing, at the same time he was trying to calm her down because she was loud. He didn't want to get his visit terminated. The C.O. chick was busted though. She had a pop belly like she was a man and was suffering from a serious case of nasatal (No ass at all).

Garnett enjoyed his visit. When he got back to the tier, he went to his sell, put the block to the door window, got some tissue, magazine, and opened the balloons and started bagging up the dope he just got.

Fee had given him the balloons on the initial kiss. He held them in his mouth the hole visit until he was about to get searched. He halfway swallowed them, then after getting searched he brought them back up. It was something he learned from one of his manz during his last bid.

For Garnett it didn't stop because he was locked up. This wasn't a lifestyle, it was his life. He was all in.

About a half an hour after he had finished bagging up it was count up. After count he went outside to the yard to serve up his usual costumers. He was trying to stay on the low so he only dealt with a few dudes, mainly white boys. One of them always wanted to take everything off of his hands. Garnett always made sure he hooked him up, but he didn't give him everything because he had other people he was dealing with.

A couple weeks later Game stopped by Fee's house. Inside the house he pulled out a pound of weed and two ounces of dope and put it on the table.

"Where you think all of that is going," Fee asked? She was more so referring to the weed because the dope wasn't any more than what she was used to taking him.

"It's going to Garnett."

"How he going to get all of that?"

"Somebody is going to come get it tomorrow night."

"Oh alright, I'll be here."

The next day around 9pm this beautiful light skin woman came knocking at the door.

"May I help you," Fee asked?

"I'm here to pick something up for Garnett."

Fee had let her in, but she couldn't help but to feel a little jealous because she knew Garnett had to be messing with her. She knew Garnett and how he was. The fact that the woman looked better than her didn't help. Fee brought the drugs downstairs, and it was like an unspoken dislike between the two, even though Fee tried her best to hide it. Lize, the other woman was polite and acted like a lady. She got what she came for and left.

Garnett worked in the ODR kitchen, so he ate a little better than the average prisoner. Lize was an ITI, which is the civilian who runs the prison kitchen to make sure all the food gets cooked. Garnett had bagged her a couple months ago. At first he had her bringing in little stuff like tapes, CD's, and phones, but then he started pushing her to bring that work in. She was refusing for a minute, but he was persistent, then she finally agreed to make a move for him.

Lize came in and put her jacket up, then went to talk to the C.O.. Fifteen minutes later that C.O. went on break and another one came in. The C.O. who had just came in went to the ODR, got some food, then went to the diner room and started eating.

"Come look out for me Mook."

When Garnett looked around the corner Lize was already gone. He hurried and rushed back there to the C.O. and civilian bathroom. When he went in there Lize was still taking everything from under her vest. Her shirt was already undone. While she was doing what she was doing he began unbuckling her pants. He pulled them down and turned her around and bent her over and started hitting it. She tried to hold her moans in as he went harder and faster. He hit it for about five minutes, bust off, then hurried to pull his pants up, grabbed the drugs then peeked out the door to ask Mook was everything clear. He came out of that bathroom and entered the inmate bathroom. Mook came in after him. Garnett started giving him some work. Southwoods was like three prisons in one, because it had three phases. Garnett was on phase one and Mook was on phase two.

Mook and Garnett had been working in the kitchen together for some months and had become the flyest of all the dudes who worked in there even though they weren't from the same city. Mook was from Newark New Jersey. He was on the phase with one of Garnett's manz, so Garnett gave Mook some work for his manz and some for himself.

"Your girl acted like she wanted to bite my head off. I guess I wasn't what she expected."

"I hope y'all don't start any bullshit. I was going to have you see ma manz, but he'll try to fuck you every time. I can't have that," Garnett said giving her a little smile.

"He wouldn't have gotten any of this."

"Yeah yeah, dudes from Camden aint like these country boys around here. Dudes from the hood apply pressure."

She didn't understand what he meant so he had to let her know how dudes from Camden was. He had seen plenty of chicks from other cities come to Camden and never leave because Camden done mess their lives up.

When Garnett talked on the phone with Fee she didn't say anything about Lize. She waited until she came up that Sunday. She bickered a little, but he didn't get into an argument with her. He just broke it down how he needed Lize to get money. Fee was upset but didn't have any choice but to accept it. Plus, he wasn't no fool, he let her know that he knew she was out there fucking. He even let her know about the dude he knew she was messing with. Of course she denied it all the way to the end. Garnett let her know he wasn't worried about it. He just knew that a lot of times females be thinking they be slick, but that don't really be the case. Garnett just really didn't care about her as much as he pretended to.

CHAPTER 6

Everybody was at the bowling alley having a good time. A few people were bowling, but it was more of a social event. A group of dudes were taking flicks, others were posted near the games. For the most part everybody was mingling, but you could see the divide in the sections of the hoods. The ladies were everywhere though.

Roy had just got his pizza. He brought this chick and her friends a couple slices. They were hanging around like they were trying to get hit so he fed them. He had already made his rounds. A few dudes who he sold weight to was there. They showed him love. Roy had became that dude, not only with females, but with dudes too. Mainly with dudes because he was the connect. On the low dudes a be trying to ease their way in to get to know him so they could get plugged in. Then there were the haters. He seen a few dudes cutting their eyes at him, but he didn't pay them any mind. Roy was neutral when it came to what part of the city he was from. That kind of made him fair game. He had dudes that would ride for him, but that was because he was feeding them or looked out at one point or another. He knew his money bought love and loyalty. That was a part of the thrill he liked about it all. Getting the attention and being able to tell people what to do.

Roy and Shon left the bowling alley with the two chicks they had bagged. When they got to the exit Roy seen Vic outside in this new light green S 560 Benz. They caught eye contact, but Roy kept it moving. He didn't want him to know that he was digging his car. Vic knew what he was doing by parking right outside the exit.

****

Daniel was used to Roy coming home every night. Some chicks knew how to play their positions, especially

47

when they were getting a free ride. When she met him, she aint have a job or a high school diploma, just a cute face and a fat ass, but that's all it take sometimes.

As soon as Roy Walked in, he smelt the eggs and grits. Daniel was over the stove doing her thing. They greeted each other with a hug and a kiss. He sat at the table, and she brought him his plate. All while eating, he kept thinking about Vic and that Benz. He wasn't feeling how Vic had stared him down. One thing he didn't like was for dudes to feel like they were better than him. He had enough money to get whatever car he wanted but he liked the Cadi truck he had.

Roy and Vic served some of the same dudes weight in the city. Even though there wasn't any beef between them there was some competition because dudes bought from whoever had the best for the lowest. A lot of times Vic got it off because Roy had to go through Fernando for his work, then he would put his price on it so he could make a profit. Ever since Fernando been locked up Roy had been dealing with Tuco directly. The result was he was able to lower his prices and ever since he been having dudes in pocket.

****

Money was coming in. Shon ran Atlantic while Roy sold weight. Tone transported some work here and there for him and got paid by the week. He was still green and was coming along slow in the game, so Roy spoon fed him. He didn't care if that was his manz or not, he was in It for self. Plus, Tone wasn't showing any real motivation. He bullshitted on the little moves Roy had him making. He probably was like that because he came from money and always had. On the other hand, Shon showed ambition. He got Roy to put Coke on Atlantic. He made it a twenty four hour flow and had his cousin Calif running it while he took a more laid back position.

Roy's whole day consisted of him going here and there to make weight sells. He felt as though he couldn't count on Tone to do everything. He really never sent him to serve real gangstas. Roy became complacent over time. He started out always having a shooter follow him to watch his back while he made deliveries. Then he began feeling like that wasn't needed. What he didn't know was a lot of real dudes seen him as soft. That meant in their eyes he was prey. Even though it was a whisper of a rumor going around that he had gotten Rasheed killed over some money. To a lot of people that didn't count because he didn't pull the trigger himself.

Roy pulled on Walnut Street downtown and waited for Chip. Chip was one of Fernando's regular weight drops, but Roy haven't seen or heard from him in a while. It was about 8pm. Roy had grown impatient, waiting around wasn't his cup of tea. He was about to pull off when a van pulled behind him. Figuring it had to be Chip he took the three bricks of coke from under the seat. In the mirror Roy could see Chip walking to the passenger side of the car. He unlocked the door and Chip got in.

"Long time no see. What's good with you," Roy asked with his hand out ready to shake Chip's hand?

"Nothing much," Chip said shaking his hand. "I aint doing much."

Tap tap tap. Roy turned around to see who was taping on his window. When he did, he seen a big barrel pointed at his face through the window.

"Roll the window down," The dude with the shotgun commanded.

Roy had heard him loud and clear. He was just shocked so it was taking him a little longer to move. Once he rolled the window down dude stuck the barrel even closer to his face. In his mind Roy was praying and hoping that dude didn't pull that trigger. This was his first time being robbed. All kind of thoughts was going through his mind. He didn't notice Chip was searching the Cadi truck. He didn't have to search hard before he found the bricks. As soon as he got them he left, the gunman did too. Once the gunman left Roy turned around and seen that Chip was gone. As the van pulled off it dawned on him that Chip had set him up. He tried to put the car in drive, but quickly realized that the keys weren't in the ignition.

That incident made him realize that respect wasn't given, that it had to be earned, even taken. That he couldn't live off of Fernando's reputation. Everyman has to have his own reputation in the streets. In order to get his own respect, he must put his own work in. He wasn't going to act like shit was sweet anymore. Selling drugs in Camden, one of the nation's most dangerous cities, making moves without a burner on you was a death wish.

Shon wasn't playing with it at all, he was getting money and doing what he do. Weed was still banging the most on Atlantic, but the coke was coming along, doing five to six thousand a shift. Knowing the block had potential to do thirty thousand a day, he had plans on pushing it to the limit. Every business needed someone like Shon, who was organized, prudent and who could get things done. In any business legal or illegal it's impossible to do everything yourself.

Shon was a couple years younger than Roy even though he looked older with full facial hair. Everything about him said grown man. Especially the way he moved. He liked to be on the low. He left the limelight to Roy and Tone. The more money he got the more he was trying to fall back. He started only going to the block when it got dark, and he always was strapped and ready

51

for action. When Roy told him how Chip robbed him, he was ready to put in work, but Roy told em that he had someone else on it. He had made a call to Jeff and him and his dudes had been hunting for Chip ever since. Shon still told Roy that if he caught Chip slipping that he was going to off him.

Roy knew Shon didn't have any problem putting in work, but he needed him for other things. It was hard to find reliable dudes that had their mind right and Roy knew this.

****

Daniel had somehow moved in with Roy even though they never officially agreed on it. He never tried to figure it out because he was always busy, and she was his girl. When he used to stay by himself, he had his apartment looking like a club house, pizza boxes on the table, trash full, piles of dirty clothes in the room. Once she started staying with him all that changed. It was always clean. Clothes always washed, she brought new furniture with his money, but he really knew she moved in when he went in the drawer to grab his boxers but the only drawers in there was her panties.

Unbeknownst to Daniel Roy had just copped a crib in Gloucester City, in a little outskirt town from Camden. He had put it in his grandmother's name. Daniel was sitting on the couch talking on the phone when he handed her the keys.

"What's these for," she asked?

"Them the keys to ya new house."

"For real? Girl, I'll call you back," she said and hung up the phone. She got up and gave Roy a hug and a kiss.

"Where we moving to?"

"Gloucester City."

Roy was getting too much money to be cooped up in the hood. Camden was surrounded by little suburban towns and on the other side of it was the Ben Franklin bridge which led to Philly. Police on the outskirts of Camden would be on some other stuff if they seen a car with Tint, rims, or if they heard loud music. That was their stereotypical way of keeping everything that goes on in Camden in Camden and out of their neighborhoods. That also made it safe for a lot of dudes who thought other dudes wouldn't cross that gun line to go get them.

Daniel fixed the house up to her liking. Roy let her do her thing and she did a good job. To him a house was just a resting place, but she made it a home. The same weekend they moved in Daniel had a housewarming party. A bunch of her family and friends came over to celebrate the fact that one of them had made it out the hood. They all brought little gifts. They were loving how Roy was treating Daniel.

"Girl he a good man. You better treat him good and not let anybody steal him from you," Daniel's aunt said. "A good man is hard to come by, especially nowadays."

Roy was walking around a house full of women. All of them bigging him up and checking him out. One of Daniel's girlfriends was giving him that look. She wasn't cute, but her body was nice. In the hood the body got more points than the face. Roy knew he could hit just by the way she was eyeing him. Later that day Roy caught her by herself.

"Why you keep looking at me like that?"

"Like what, I was just looking," she said.

"Nah, you looking like you want something. Look, meet me at Fresh Donuts at nine and I'll give you what you looking for."

Later that night Roy was riding down Haddon Ave when he got pulled over by the police. Roy tucked his gun underneath of the back seat.

"Driver license, registration and proof of insurance."

When Roy couldn't provide his license he was asked to step out of the vehicle. He was searched, put into the back of the cop car, then his truck was searched. They found the gun and he was locked up.

****

Garnett was doing his thing. He had his phase sowed up and some of the other phases. Not too many dudes were getting it in like him. Ever since Lize started bringing it in for him he been having her bring in a lot more. She was playing her part to the fullest and she didn't ask much of him.

The prison was filled with gangs. Garnett wasn't into any of that, but he sold weight to a few dudes who was the heads of that. He also dealt with a couple dudes from Camden and some white boys. He was making moves like every two to three weeks giving dudes money enough time to land.

One blood dude had tried to play him. He had to set an example for everybody to see. Dude had G under one of them sets, Garnett didn't care about any of that. He gave him two bricks of dope (Street bags) and dude money never got to Garnett's spot. Not trying to sweat dude Garnett waited like a month before approaching dude in the yard. O boy started getting loud, coming out of his face the wrong way, putting on a show for his boys. Garnett sent a right straight down the pike. Dude slid down the wall snoring. The guys around him looked in awe. Garnett looked at them to see if they wanted any work, but it was clear they didn't.

Garnett was getting short, he didn't have time for the bs. He was trying to get his head together and come up with a plan. Even after he went to the county and made bail, he knew that he was going to have to come back to prison. It was no chance of him getting time served because he was too short and once he hit the county that was over. His lawyer said he might have to do about three and a half years. Garnett wasn't really trying to do any time, so he planned on postponing his court dates as long as he could.

A few months later he maxed out his parole and got detained to the county where he bailed out. It was nighttime when he got processed out. Fee must have thought that he was going to be beasting to get his nuts out of the sand, but they were never really in the sand because the whole time up state he was smashing Lize.

Garnett and Lize had good chemistry. She was some other type of chick, suburban, green, square chick that didn't know it. They were the total opposites which was probably why they got along so good.

"Where my baby at," Garnett asked Fee when he got in the house?

"I sent her to ya sister Lima's house so we could get our freak on."

"I don't want none of you, I want to see ma baby girl."

"You're starting ya bs already."

Fee wanted sex and wasn't trying to let him leave the house until she got some. She went to change into some lingerie that she had bought just for when he got home. She knew what he liked. The Lingerie was white see through lace top with little red details and white see through panties.

Garnett came upstairs when she called him. She started taking his clothes off, he let her. Once naked he sat on the bed, she started sucking him off. She stopped and they got all the way on the bed. She rode him until he came. He wasn't into it how she was, so he was one and done. His excuse was that he had to get used to it again. She understood because she thought he hadn't had any since he been gone. The truth was that he could tell that somebody had been tampering with her cookie because that thing was loose than a goose. It had to be someone who was bigger than him, so his pride was kind of hurt.

"I hope you done with dude you was letting smash while I was gone."

"I wasn't messing with anybody."

"Stop lying, because that's going to make me stop trusting you all together. Just know you disrespect me I'm going to shoot you, not him."

****

A couple of Garnett's friends had hit him off and took him shopping. Typical stuff when a real one was back on the scene, and he got real ones out there. Garnett dived right back into the mix headfirst like he never left. The guy Duke he caught the charge with been home. He had bailed out the next day.

Garnett, Game, J.B., and T-Roy was set up to pull a mission on this dude from Parkside name Rich. Game was to meet dude on 9th and Mechanic. When Rich showed up Game was already waiting. He pulled a couple cars a head of Game, got out and as soon as he closed his car door, he heard a shot and felt like he was hit. He squatted near his car, looked up, he seen three dudes coming from the train tracks masked up. He took off running. Two of them chased him while the others went for his car. They got him for two bricks of coke.

That robbery took place in the early afternoon. Around 9:30 at night on 8th street out Centerville it was packed. Guys and girls just out there enjoying themselves. Three cars of Rich's dudes came through and jumped out. The first shot was a loud blast. That had to had come from a shotty. T-Roy never seen it coming and he didn't need to because it was ugly. From how it twisted him he had to be dead on impact.

From there it was Ak, Sk, Ar-15, all big shots ringing off echoing through the projects. The masked men ran through the crowd aiming for all dudes. Four bodies dropped, and a couple others were shot. Garnett got away unscathed. The only one who got killed that had anything to do with that robbery was T-Roy.

With everything that went on in Camden it rarely made the news, but that night it did which made Centerville hot. They couldn't really get money how they wanted to after that.

Garnett and his dudes had slept on Rich because he was a skinny light skin dude with glasses. He didn't look the part of a regular gangsta from the hood, but he was definitely a G and a major figure in Parkside.

****

Roy had been bailed out on that gun charge. Days after he got out, he copped a dark purple S 560 Benz. He had gotten the car in his grandmother's name. She haven't had a job in years, but her credit was good. That purple may sound fruity, but the car was a beauty. Everywhere he went he turned heads. Them three bricks he got robbed for aint do anything but put a little dent in his stash. It wasn't anything that was going to set him back. He let Chip and his nut ass boys know that when he rode through Sycamore courts doing about five miles per hour. Chip wasn't out there but some of his boys were, so Roy knew that he'll hear about it. He rode fishbowl, he wanted everybody to see who was driving it. It was his way of giving all the haters the middle finger.

Roy opened an autobody shop on Kaighn Ave. He was trying to make business moves. His bricks were coming twenty five at a time. He was moving them like it was nothing. His auto body shop took off immediately. Somebody always needed their car fixed. He sold rims, tires, and car radio systems on the inside. He also made a lot of transactions there. For that reason, the guys he had working there stayed strap.

Roy had stop messing with Tone. He was messing up money, not little amounts either. He was given multiple opportunities, but he didn't seem to have it in him. He wasn't a hustler. When Roy cut him off, he had told him that the game wasn't for him.

Randy walked in the shop around his appointed time. Roy had been waiting in his office. His manz knocked, then opened the door, letting Randy in.

"What's up big guy," Randy said addressing Roy.

"Nothing much, how's everything?"

"Business as usual. You still be dealing with Tone?"

"Nah, he still cool but I had to leave him alone as far as business is concerned."

"Well, he must didn't get the message because he sold ma peoples something and said that it came from you and it lost grams."

"Oh yeah, thanks for letting me know. Let ya peoples know that it didn't come from me. If he want that proper work tell him to get at me though."

After Roy and Tone stop dealing with each other Tone was still making moves, but he was getting work from somewhere else trying to serve the clientele that he got from Roy as if what he had was still coming from him. Tone and his peoples had some bad coke, so Roy was getting calls finding out that Tone was still making moves in his name. Roy couldn't afford that. He gave tone a call about it, but Tone kept denying it.

"I aint telling nobody I got ya shit."

"We'll stop contacting ma peoples then."

"They still contacting me so I'm going to serve them."

"Why you trying to sound hardbody? You know that aint you."

"Fuck what you talking about, this me. Don't let ya money go to ya head. You still just Roy in ma eyes."

"Alright, whatever tough guy, just stop doing what you doing," Roy said before hanging up.

It's true what they say about money being able to mess up friendships. Beef wasn't declared when they got off of the phone, but it was clear that the love was gone. The next time they seen each other it was a quick stare, no what's up or anything. Tone was doing his thing but most of his flow was dudes he was dealing with from when he was selling weight for Roy.

****

July 17 was Roy's birthday, Daniel had threw him a party at this club in A.C.. Everybody who was somebody or who thought they were somebody from Camden came. Daniel's friend from the housewarming party was there too. She had this little red skirt on. Roy could tell she didn't have on any panties. She was still giving him that look.

Roy looked around for Daniel and spotted her at the bar. He went over to her friend Shamera and told her to meet him in the bathroom. No later than a minute she came in there and he took her in the stall. He lifted that skirt up, put one leg up and started hitting it.

They had got a quicky in and snuck back to the party without anyone missing them.

Everybody knew how hard Parkside and Centerville was beefing, so when Garnett and his dudes arrived the tension was felt. Parkside dudes was already in there. It didn't take long for a brawl to break out. Luckily nobody had any guns on them in there, but they were rocking out and dudes were getting smacked and stabbed with bottles.

****

The next day Garnett showed up to Roy's auto body shop.

"I apologize bro, we didn't mean to mess your day up. I feel bad about that."

"Ya'll tore that spot up. I had to pay for that too."

Garnett had cuts and bruises on his face and hands, he didn't care though.

"Ya'll put the security guard in the hospital."

"Fuck him, I was hoping one of them other dudes was in the hospital."

"I hear that but look, I need you to put some work in for me," Roy said as they stepped to the side where nobody could hear them. "What's the price?"

Garnett stared at him. "You want dude Chip handled? I heard he did some bs."

"He broke mentally, so he'll be back on a ounce where he belong. You can't turn a two thousand dollar man into a two hundred thousand dollar man, he just going to go back to that two thousand. Not him though, I got something for him. I need you to get at Tone for me."

"You talking about ya manz?"

"We don't deal with each other anymore, he a snake."

"I know how it is. For twenty thousand I'll bring you his head."

"Nah, just put a hole in it for me."

Roy went in his office and came out with the twenty thousand. Two stacks of ten thousand. Garnett thought he was going to get half up front and half when the mission was complete. Roy didn't play around, he gave him all the money from the door and expected him to do what he said he was going to do.

Garnett jumped on the job immediately. Tone stayed on the move, but he was local. Riding with Game he spotted him at Rita's on Mt. Ephraim Ave talking to somebody. Garnett aint tell any of his dudes that he had a contract. He told Game to take him to his car. Once in his car he rode back to where Tone was. He parked his car behind Bonsall School, masked up and started walking up the street. Rita's was on the corner. Garnett got to the top of the street turned and Tone was right there facing dude he was talking to. Garnett put the 45. To the back of his head and didn't waste any time pulling the trigger. BOOM! Garnett's arm jerked back. The bullet went in one side of Tone's head and exited the other side. He was dead but his body took a few seconds before it fell over like a tree that had been cut down in the woods. The bullet had just missed dude he was talking too. As soon as dude heard the shot, he took off running.

Garnett like many other dudes in Camden was living in a state of I don't give a fuck. In this state dudes weren't human. They were worse than animals. Mortality wasn't a thought. It was eat or be eaten. Survival of the fittest, life didn't have any value.

Chapter 7

When Tuco found out that his nephew had got murdered he called Roy to find out what was going on.

"A lot of bs been going on lately," he told Tuco.

Tuco wanted to know who did it so he could get some revenge. Their family had been tested over the years and it was times that they had to set examples to let people know that they couldn't do something to them and just get away with it.

"Don't worry, I'm going to find out who did it and take care of it," Roy tried to assure Tuco.

At Tone's funeral Tuco came with two guys. They stood silent and followed him closely everywhere he went. Even when he spoke to them in Spanish, they only answered back in one or two words. They were real militant.

"You handle that yet," Tuco asked Roy?

Roy knew he was talking about getting at the person who killed Tone. Roy looked at Tone's casket. It was people in line to view his corps. He knew somebody had to pay, but definitely not him.

"Nah, I aint make it happen yet," Roy responded. "I got it though. I know who did it."

"Alright, I'ma leave you some help. They're going to handle everything, just show them who."

Having two dudes who he didn't know follow him around all day everyday was very uncomfortable at first, but he decided to use them the same way Tuco was using them, as bodyguards.

They kept going through Sycamore in a tinted up van that dudes out there didn't know. Every time they went out there dudes was out there trapping, but Chip wasn't out there. That was to Roy's disappointment because he knew the two papi dudes wasn't leaving until they completed their mission.

"That look like him right there," Roy said in Spanish. The two papi dudes had AK 47's. Roy was parked down the street from Sycamore courts when he seen Chip. That's when he pulled off going at regular speed. "That's him with the green jacket and black hoodie on."

Other dudes were out there two, but they would more than likely become collateral damage. Roy pulled to the corner and the two dudes got out of the car and began walking like they were in the army. Civilians were scrambling to get out of their way as they made no attempts to hide their faces or the big ass guns they were carrying.

"They got guns," a women yelled out.

They knew enough English to know that she had just gave them up because they went into action. About ten feet from where Chip stood they started trying to gun him down. Everyone started running and firing back, but the two dudes made no attempts to hide or dodge the shots that came back at them. Chip was shooting back at the guys who chased him. The shots from his 9mm sounded like a firecracker compared to them AK shots. They chased him until he ran out of bullets. He ran on somebody's porch, and they lit him up. They both went on the porch and stood over him to finish him off.

All Roy heard was shots. He was nervous as ever. He sat low in the car checking all the mirrors and kept looking around. He was hoping that they came running around the corner at any second. It took a little longer than he thought, but when they did turn the corner, they were walking causally with them big guns in their hands like they were in a third world country. "These mothafuckas are crazy," Roy said to himself. He started flagging them to hurry up, but they just kept strolling. They might of didn't care about going to jail but he did.

A few shots rang off, it sounded like it came from a 22. or a 25. They both lifted their guns up and let loose. Roy put the car in drive and rode up to them. They got in and he put the pedal to the medal.

That night a couple of people had gotten shot. One dude died on the block, Chip got killed and an old lady got grazed in the arm by a stray bullet. Roy was more than glad for them dudes to go back to Puerto Rico or wherever Tuco had brought them in from. He wasn't sure if they were there to kill him too or what. Not knowing if Tuco really bought his story about how Tone got killed had him shook. Especially while them two goons were in town. He had told Tuco that Chip had robbed them and when Tone seen him, he started shooting at him and that Chip caught him slipping. That's all he could come up with at the time, but it worked. He felt even more relieved because he killed two birds with one stone.

The streets have ways of putting the puzzles together. It was becoming known that Roy wasn't to be messed with. He thought he was moving on the low until he got picked up by the detectives and took to the police station for questioning.

"I don't know what ya'll talking about, that was like my brother."

The detectives were questioning him about Tone's murder. Whoever they were getting their information from knew what they were talking about, but they didn't have proof.

"Just to let you know this aint the first time your name came up involved in something." The detective didn't say what his name had come up in. Roy looked at him with a blank stare waiting to hear if he was going to tell him or not, but that was all he said.

When Roy got home Daniel had company over. Tish and Shamera, it was normal for Daniel to have company over, it just felt funny being as though he had smashed Shamera. It was definitely not a coincidence, but he greeted them, and they greeted him back. He went in the kitchen, then upstairs so they could have their girls gathering.

****

"What's up with ya manz Roy," Game asked Garnett?

"Nah, we aint getting him, that's ma dude."

"I aint talking about that, I'm talking about copping some coke from him."

"Oh, he definitely got them things. I'ma see what's up for you."

"I don't want to meet him. I'ma go through you."

"Why you don't want to meet him," Garnett asked?

"It's just something about him. Me personally, I don't think he like that, but that's ya manz so I rather go through you since you trust him."

"You think he'll snitch," Garnett asked curious to know what Game was seeing that he wasn't?

"I never heard anything like that, but I don't think he'll hold up if the situation presents itself. He just look like a rat. Even his facial structure. That's what he reminds me of when I see him."

Garnett started laughing, but Game was dead serious. Roy and Game knew of one another but have never met.

"Alright, he look funny. I aint into liking dudes so I could care less how he look. If he go cop on anybody it's going to be his self because he be doing a lot of dirt."

"He don't do dirt himself, he make his money work for him."

"Same difference, what he going to say, I got such and such to kill him for me," Garnett said being sarcastic. "When you reach a certain status you aint going to be getting your hands dirty either."

"I'm always going to put ma own work in," Game said sure of himself.

****

When Garnett left from with Game he went to his sister Irene's house. His other sister Lima was there also. All his nieces and nephews came running up to him asking him for money. It was five of them. They all swarmed him, hugging on his leg and tugging on his arm. That made him feel good. Even though they were asking for money he felt real love coming from the little ones. He pulled out a big no fold and started giving them money. Once they got what they came for they all

71

dispersed. He put his money back in his pockets, but he knew it was only a matter of time before his sister hit him up.

"Lima, did you find out if she still dealing with dude?"

"If she is, she's creeping because I aint been hearing anything. I'm on it though bro."

Lima was the one who told Garnett Fee was messing with Umar while he was locked up. Since they were friends, he had her trying to find out if they were still messing around since he'd been home.

"What you got going on," Lima asked?

"You know me, just trying to stay alive. What you got to eat in here," Garnett asked Irene on his way to the kitchen? He grabbed some grape juice and Cheetos and sat down. Irene was at the table doing Lima's hair.

"You know Kelly mess with one of them Parkside dudes ya'll beefing with. He be staying over there a lot too."

"Which one is it?"

"His name Poog."

"I never heard of him. Is he somebody out there?"

"I think he is. He act like it anyway."

"I never heard of dude, but I'ma talk to ma peoples to find out about him."

If Poog was just a packman he wasn't going to go out of his way to get at him. Garnett only got people he felt counted.

"Where Kelly stay?"

"She lives in Crestbury. "

Chestbury was better known as Lurkybury, because a lot of smuts had apartments out there and dudes would get caught lurking out there on the regular coming in and out of one of their apartments.

"I wanted some of Kelly fat ass too. She out there sleeping with the enemy, huh?"

There was a knock at the door. Garnett got up and answered it. In came his other sister Lola with her friend Peach. They came in extra loud. Peach was trying to flirt with Garnett while Lola rolled up some weed. They started talking about different dudes and Garnett was ear hustling getting the scoop on everybody they were talking about. He knew in a way he was blowing their shit because they couldn't say what they really wanted to say because he was their brother.

"Yeah girl, I be messing with Brees now."

"You talking about Brees from Whiteboy Fairview?"

"Yup, I got that. He spends money too," Peach said.

Garnett was sitting there thinking that whoever was spending on this silly chick was suffering from a case of bitch dependency. Peach was all in his face, his sisters were hood rats and so were their friends. Peach being in his face wasn't doing much for him. In the hood the roles were reversed, hood rat chicks got more points for having sex with a real dude than he would get for having sex with her. He was somebody, she was just a bucket. Garnett was always ready to play though.

"What are you going to do with that," Garnett asked after he whipped out?

Peach grabbed it and was about to go down on him.

"What ya'll doing over there. Take that shit upstairs before the kids come back in," his sister yelled.

Peach led him upstairs to the bathroom where she commenced to polish his Oscar.

****

Meanwhile on the other side of town Fee was on her knees sucking Umar all crazy. She had his toes curling. He grabbed the back of her head and started fucking her mouth, ramming it down her throat. When he bust off, she swallowed everything.

Dudes like Garnett didn't think stuff like that could happen to him. He felt like he was too gangsta. That any chick who dealt with him knew better, but obviously that wasn't the case. Dealing with women was a whole different game.

Fee came up kissing Umar's on his Pelvis, stomach, chest and then his lips. Then they laid there holding each other like a couple.

Chapter 8

A car pulled in the alley between Atlantic and Lansdowne. Caleaf ran up to the car with his stash in his hand.

"Let me get eight youngen," the fiend in the driver seat said. It was two of them. Caleaf got the money and walked off counting it. When he got out of the alley and into the light, he seen that they had given him four fake twenty dollar bills. He pulled his burner out and started shooting at their car. Shon and leak had ran over there with their guns out.

"What happened," Shon asked?

"These fiends played me, gave me these fake twenties."

"Come on, let's get out of here before them boys come," Shon said.

They shut down shop for the day. A couple hours later they got up with Roy and Shon had put them on to what happened. They were riding around in Roy's Benz.

"Don't give them twenties to the connect, you fuck around and get killed like that," Roy joked with Caleaf.

"Nah, I wasn't," Caleaf responded.

"I'm playing with you anyway. I'm serious about not passing them on, but I was just joking with you. I'ma show you how to spend them."

They went over Philly to this strip club called The Purple Orchid. They were in there drinking, talking and watching the girls dance on stage. A couple strippers came over there flirting with them. Roy already put Caleaf on how to get rid of them. Caleaf found this stripper that he wanted to hit. They went to this little room where he got his rocks off. He paid her a hundred and twenty altogether. Most of it was with them fake twenties.

Caleaf was up and coming. Out of all the other dudes he was the one that stood out because he was thorough and liked to get to the money. That's why he was running the block, not just because he was Shon's cousin.

One day Shon and Roy was riding around when Shon suggested opening up on Princess and Bradley. It was an old vacant set that nobody was laying claim to. Roy gave him the green light and they expanded over there.

****

Christmas came around and Roy and Daniel spent theirs in the house together. They had a little tree. Roy filled it up with all these gifts. She bought him a few things. Every time she opened a gift he got a hug and a kiss. He felt proud to make her happy. Daniel was playing her part. Whatever her history was in the past, it didn't matter because she was showing him nothing but good qualities.

"I got one last present for you," Daniel said. She got up and went in the room. Roy thought she was about to change into something sexy for em. That was the first place his mind went. She was wearing something different when she came out but nothing like he was expecting. She stood in front of him, took his hand and placed it on her belly. He had a surprised look on his face.

"This is my present to you," she said.

"Really, that's my baby in there?"

Roy stood up and gave her a big hug and kiss. That night they made love in front of the Christmas tree.

****

Garnett finally got up with Roy and they started making moves. Out of Garnett's squad he was the only one who dealt with Roy. When it was time to re-up his dudes would give him the money and he would get up with Roy. Every time he would cop Roy would front him a few extra, depending on what he copped. He did that to keep Garnett dealing with him. Roy knew he had other connects so he was trying to keep him on the hook.

After the holidays had passed Roy had went downtown to see his lawyer. He waited in the lobby while his lawyer met with another client. This old lady came out of the office with her teenage son. The boy looked like he was a troubled youth in the streets doing things he shouldn't be doing and had got caught.

"Mr. Mckinnie, Mr. Gilbert will see you now."

Roy got up and went in his lawyer's office. On entering his lawyer hung up the phone.

"How are you today Mr. Mckinnie," Mr. Gilbert asked as he stood up and extended his reach over the desk to shake Roy's hand?

"I'm good, how about yourself?"

"Working," his lawyer said.

"How is things going with my case?"

"Oh, you're going to be good. It's your first adult charge. I'm going to try to get you probation. You got a court date fooooor……" He began checking his calendar. "For March 16, we're going to handle everything then."

"Alright thanks," Roy said as he got out of his seat.

"Mr. Mckinnie, would you like to come to a gathering with me?"

"A gathering," Roy asked?

"It's something like a party, but the kind of people I'm around we don't call it that. We call them gatherings."

I hope this dude aint on no gay shit, Roy thought to himself while his lawyer was still talking.

"I could introduce you to some people who you might need down the line if you know what I mean."

"I'll take you up on that, when is it?"

"Friday, here is the address."

He gave Roy a piece of paper. Roy seen it was a Cherry Hill address. That was close. He couldn't help but to wonder what kind of gathering it would be. On his way out Roy heard the secretary say bye in a seductive way. At first, he didn't pay it any mind but as he got in his car her tone dawn on him. Plus, he kept thinking about how she was looking at him.

****

Friday night Roy arrived at the mansion. It was a lot of cars parked along the wrap around driveway. He dressed causal in some slacks, hard bottoms and a nice shirt. He didn't wonna overdo it and look like a pimp. He didn't know what kind of gathering it was. From the looks of the tags on the cars he knew he was out of pocket. All the cars had state and government issued tags. He gave the valet his keys, when he got to the door man the door man checked the list and let him in.

Once in Roy looked around thinking how he had to be the youngest person there. Especially out of the men. There were some young women there. For the most part all the guys looked to be in a range from mid thirties to late sixties.

"Mr. Mckinnie," Roy heard a lovely Familiar voice say. He turned around and seen his lawyer's secretary with a drink in her hand looking stunning. "I'm sorry, I never got a chance to introduce myself. My name is Amy Bosworth. Come on, Mr. Gilbert is expecting you."

She led him to where Mr. Gilbert was. Roy couldn't but help to notice the curious looks he was getting. They only added to him really feeling out of place, but he tried not to think anything of it. So far, he only seen two black people there.

Mr. Gilbert was talking to a fat stubby guy until he seen Roy coming. "Royal McKinnie, my friend," Mr. Gilbert excitedly said. He gave Roy a firm handshake and embraced him like they were boys.

It was obvious he had a drink or two, but he had also had a few bumps of that white stuff.

"Royal McKinnie, this is judge Hilton. Judge Hilton this is my friend Royal McKinnie. He's a good guy," he said as if he was secretly trying to tell the judge something.

In Roy's mind he was thinking, *Judge, friend.* He became a little stiff because it was rare for any hood dude to be around a judge at a gathering or anywhere besides a courtroom fighting for his freedom. Consciously he tried to turn down his hood swag and be a little proper. He tried to talk with a little sophistication. Him and the judge shook hands and got to talking. Roy was kind of surprised to see how down to earth Judge Hilton really was.

"Would you like a cigar Mr. McKinnie," the Judge asked?

81

"Sure, why not," Roy responded.

The Judge gave both Roy and Mr. Gilbert a Cuban cigar.

"These are the best. Their Cubans, that makes them illegal which makes me smoke them more because I am the law, Ha Ha ha."

The Judge busted out in a big hearty laugh. Mr. Gilbert laughed, and Roy followed suit. He didn't want to be the odd ball out. Roy noticed that his lawyer's eyes were unusually red. He knew that couldn't have come from just drinks alone. His lawyer turned him around a little and began introducing him to more of his colleagues. They range from other lawyers, to prosecutors, to judges, even an assistant D.A.. They all weren't from Camden County. Some were from the surrounding counties.

"Tell me what do you see when you look around?"

"I see your secretary keep eyeing me over there," Roy said talking about Amy who was across the room looking at them.

"Besides her, what else do you see?"

"I see a lot of authority figures and I feel out of place."

"Why do you feel out of place. I'm introducing you to connections and resources. Your supposed to be able to work these types of rooms. You having access to these people means you have access to power. Now of course you're going to have to grease some palms, but one of the good things is that most of them like to party if you know what I mean."

"Party, like get high," Roy asked?

"Yeah, sniff coke and trick. Them looks you was getting wasn't the evil eye, that was admiration, you're the man. It might take a while for you to get used to dealing with my kind of people because they're the law, but I got you. You just have to promise one thing."

"What's that?"

"That you keep all of this to yourself."

"No problem," Roy said.

That night Roy couldn't sleep thinking of his experience. He was trying to figure out how he was going to make the best of it. He knew he had to fall back from being so close to the streets. At the same time step his game up. Money was good, but it could always get better.

Chapter 9

For Valentine's Day Roy and Daniel went to the Poconos Mountains for three days. The trip provided Roy with some relief. A chance to relax and take his mind off of things. Camden city was full court pressure, twenty four hours, seven days a week. Anything could happen at any given time, which made it like a war zone. In the position Roy was in he had to always be on point.

****

Shon was stepping his game up. He handled Roy's weight sells while he was gone, Caleaf was running Atlantic. John John, one of their other young boys was running Princess and Bradley. Everything went smooth. While Roy was gone Shon realized that he wasn't feeling the weight game at all. He had to deal with too many dudes, that wasn't his thing. It was too many dudes knowing his business and too many dudes that could possibly rat on him. He couldn't wait to pass the torch back to Roy.

****

Roy showed up to court ready to get it over with. He waited in the waiting room until his lawyer showed up. He said a couple words to Roy then went in the court room. Not soon after the Sheriff called Roy's name. Roy went in the court room. When the judge came out it was Judge Hilton. Roy looked over at the prosecutor's table and remembered seeing her that night also. After everything was said he left out with six months probation. He didn't think much of it because he felt like he would have got probation anyway beings as though it was his only adult charge.

****

"I'm no tolerance, no nonsense, you screw up I won't have a problem violating you. I'm going to urine test you randomly etc...."

His probation officer went on explaining the rules and regulations. It wasn't what he said, it was how he said it that made Roy know that he was dick head.

****

Garnett was in the hood getting money and robbing dudes that he felt wasn't supposed to be eating anyway. Him and his dudes wasn't into robbing dudes on the corners trapping packs. They ran in houses for bricks and did the kidnap thing. Depending on who the person was or how they did it determined rather that person lived or not. Most dudes didn't live though. The whole hood knew how they played. A lot of times they got blamed for things they didn't even do, just because of their reputation. Needless to say, they stayed in a lot of beef.

They had a caper set on this dude Shakur from East on Randolph Street. Dude was getting money. They had heard from a little birdy that he was holding work over Face cousin Meme house. Face was another one of Garnet's manz.

Shakur was in the house. Face knew the blueprint to the house like the back of his hand. There weren't any lights on. Face figured they must have been in the bedroom. Meme had one of them old back doors with the little square window on it. Face led the pack since it was his cousin's crib. He broke out one of the little windows and stuck his hand in there to open the door. Garnett, Game and JB went in masked up with their guns in hand. Face led them through the house creeping.

"Oh, oh harder, harder, come on," they heard as they crept up the steps. Shakur was pounding Meme out, but she was taking it like a champ, encouraging him to go harder. They stood at the door for a couple of seconds watching. Face started feeling some type of way. He grabbed dude by the neck and yanked him out of the pussy.

"What the fuck," Shakur said shocked.

Face had the burner to his face. Meme began yelling, JB tried shutting her up.

"Shut the fuck up if you wonna live," he told her.

Face had already told them not to do anything to his cousin. He didn't say anything about not scaring her.

"Where is it mothafucka, everything," Garnett said with aggression in his voice?

Face wasn't talking because Meme might recognize his voice.

"It's in the closet," Shakur said.

Game and Garnett searched the closet and came out with a brick and what looked like another half. Three handguns and some money. They tied both of them up and made their getaway.

****

Even though Garnett was on bail he still rode around with his gun on his lap. Better to get caught with it than without it then without it was his motto. He was making his court appearances and planned on postponing things for as long as he could. He knew when the time came that they were going to have to catch him, of course his lawyer didn't know that.

Garnett was still dealing with Lize. Chilling with her helped him get away from the hood. She lived in Vineland. It was rural out there, nobody knew em. She was a different kind of chick than Fee, in her manners and in the way she lived. She still was a freak though and the truth of the matter was he didn't give a fuck about her, just like he didn't give a fuck about anybody else. The only person he felt he owed anything to was his daughter. He made sure she didn't want for anything, but he was married to the streets.

Garnett and his dudes had so much beef that they couldn't just walk the streets like regular people could. The main beef they had was with dudes from Parkside because their manz had gotten killed.

Months went by since they tried to rob Rich. The beef was far from over, but either side was on some young boy stuff, shooting blocks up, making things hot. It was whoever got caught slipping would face the firing squad.

A couple of dudes from Garnett's block had came to Fresh Donuts after the club had let out. None of them was of the hierarchy, but because they were from out there and they were out of pocket. There was a bunch of people out there in the parking lot. Across the street was an apartment that the younger dudes from Parkside be in. They were looking out the window and spotted them. Two young boys came from out the back and stood right across the street from the crowd unnoticed. The crowd continued their after party. The young boys started letting off shots, emptying their clips then hauled assed.

Garnett was over Philly when he received a call from his young boy.

"Alright, handle that then. Go earn ya stripes," Garnet told him before hanging up. He wasn't with holding hands. Everybody had to put in their fair share of work. If he wasn't there things still should get handled.

When Garnett got back to the hood, he got rushed with the news of what happened, but he wasn't worried about it at all. His mind was on his re-up. Later that day he went to Roy's shop, but Roy wasn't there, he had to deal with his manz Sam.

Chapter 10

Roy's mom Keisha walked through the door of his grandmom's house. She was probably the only black person who had permission to do so. Roy's grandmom treated her like she was family. Keisha still looked good to be an old head. She stayed dolled up and her ass was still fat.

"There go my baby," she said referring to Roy. Him, his grandmom and his fat girl cousin were at the table eating and talking. His mom came in hugging everyone.

"Go on and get yourself a plate," Roy's grandmom said inviting Keisha to join them.

Keisha had went to make a plate and came back and sat next to Roy. This was the first time he ate with his mom in years. They had a good diner. They talked about a little of everything. Even about Roy's lady Daniel and the man in Keisha's life. They agreed to one day double date so they could get to meet them.

****

Daniel's stomach was looking like it was about to pop. Only a month and a half left, and Roy would get to meet his daughter. The closer the baby got to being here the more in love Daniel seem to be with Roy. She always wanted him around so she could be touchy feely. He was staying home with her more than he used too. When he wasn't there, she would call her friends over to keep her company. Shamera was more than happy to come over, some nights staying the night. Depending on how he felt he would creep with her. Daniel was a heavy sleeper, and she went to bed early so it didn't take much for them to creep. Beside that Daniel would get him to go Baby shopping with her, which blew his mood because they would end up shopping for more than the baby and they'll be there for hours, but he loved Daniel and was trying to do his best to be a family man.

****

"You got any brothers like you," Daniel's cousin asked?

"Nah, I don't have any brothers," Roy replied.

"I know you got some cousins or friends. Hook me up with somebody," she said.

"I'ma see what I can do for you," Roy said just to get her out of his face.

Daniel was having a baby shower. There was a crowded house with family and friends. Roy stayed for a little but made an early exit.

****

Roy and Daniel had met his mom and her dude at a restaurant in Cherry Hill.

"Allllll, that's my grand baby in there," Keisha said as she got up to hug Daniel. She put her hand on Daniel's belly and began rubbing it for what she believed was good luck. Roy shook her dude's hand and introduced himself. They all got acquainted while they ate. Keisha was the star of the show, she kept everyone entertained.

Keisha had shut down the Black Barbie House, she was on another phase of her life. Roy was proud of her because she was doing good and was happy. Her dude Don seemed cool too. He must didn't know about her past because he seem content. He was a little older than Keisha. Roy could tell from the way he dressed and his car that he had money. Plus, he didn't see his mother being happy with him if he didn't. As they talked it came out that he was some type of corporate dude. Roy knew that his mom done found her a sucka.

****

Roy was on his way back from Philly when he received a call letting him know Daniel was in labor. He rushed to Our Lady of Lords where she was. Once there he told them who he was. They put him in some blue Scrubs and a mask, then took him into the delivery room. Daniel was in the mist of giving birth, before he got to the room, he could hear her screaming. He walked in the delivery room and seen her legs open and a doctor in between them ready to receive the baby. The doctor was blocking his view. When Roy stepped in for a closer look he passed out.

Roy woke up in the hospital bed right next to Daniel. They brought him the baby as if he was the one who just gave birth. Roy laid there holding the baby, Daniel laughed at seeing him like that.

The doctor began talking to Daniel. He was telling her how she needed to wait six weeks before having sex. When Roy heard him say that he took his eyes from admiring the baby and glanced over there thinking, that she needed to wait more than six weeks after he seen how wide that thing opened up.

Chapter 11

Mr. Gilbert had told Roy about the up coming gathering. It was something they did every few months. A few of the people Roy met from the first meeting he attended he still had on the hip buying ounces of coke from him. At times when requested he would hook his peoples up with a couple of around the way girls, he knew who like to play for a couple dollars.

Roy pulled up to the same mansion his lawyer invited him to before. He got out with a suitcase in his hand as if he was there to conduct business. He tipped the valet and the door man. This time when he went in there everybody was trying to speak and get a few words in with him. Through word of mouth, he had become more known than he had knew. He gave his lawyer the suitcase he was carrying, and they went and did what they did. Before Roy knew it the whole party was coked up.

Roy excused himself from a conversation he was having with these two gentlemen. On his way to the bathroom, he heard a female making sex noises. He peeked his head in the room and seen that it was a lawyer and a prosecutor getting it in. He was rabbit jabbing, and she was going crazy. Roy just smiled and kept going about his business.

When he came back to the bar Amy walked up to him.

"Are you enjoying your night Mr. Mckinnie?"

"Of course, I am. All of this is entertainment for me." For Roy seeing all of them prominent people act out of character was pure entertainment. "How about you, are you enjoying yourself?"

"Sort of, it gets old after a while. These old men getting drugged up and drooling over you. Kind of creepy, you know. I need to be chilling with you," Amy said rubbing his leg.

Roy instantly got hard and began looking at Amy in a different light. Naturally he wasn't attracted to white women, but in a blink of an eye all that had changed. He was now noticing her cleavage and the short skirt she wore. She kept talking like she wanted it, so they went up stairs and found a room, but upon entering they seen that it was already being occupied by three people having sex. One of the judges Roy had met was standing up jerking off, watching a female get hit from the back by another guy. Roy didn't get a chance to see who they were because as soon as he opened the door and seen a dude standing there, he quickly closed it and excused himself.

The next room they found was empty. They began kissing, he palmed her little cheeks and squeezed them.

She was hot and horny. She sat on the edge of the bed and pulled down her thong and lifted her skirt. Roy pulled out and got between them thighs and started stroking.

****

Everything was looking up for Roy. Being connected to Judges and prosecutors made him feel untouchable. His operation was expanding. He was making a lot of money. He tried to keep everyone satisfied, the people working for him as well as his connections. The only person who was blowing his stuff was his probation officer. What made it worse was one time when Roy had went to probation and his officer seen what he pulled up in.

"I see you drive a Mercedes Benz Mr. McKinnie. What are you some kind of drug dealer? Where do you work?"

"I own an auto Mechanic shop," Roy said with a smile on his face.

"How did you get that," Mr. Huffman asked as if he wasn't going to believe anything Roy said no way.

"I worked hard and saved my money. You should try it, maybe you won't be so bitter."

"Watch it Mr. Smart Ass, before I have you in prison fighting for your manhood."

Roy didn't respond. When he went to probation his attentions was to get in and get out as fast as he could, but his probation officer always gave him a hard time. Once he was out of there, he figured that it was time to test some of his powers out on this ball buster. The last place he wanted to do was end up in a jam. He called his friend, Judge Hilton and told him about the matter. Judge Hilton told him not to worry, that he'll take care of everything.

Chapter 12

Caleaf saw this dude make a couple of sells right down the street. Even though it wasn't directly on the set, it was close enough for dude to be in violation.

"Yo, come here money," Caleaf yelled walking real fast towards dude.

"What's good," dude asked? Him and his manz just stood there. They didn't look like they were scared either.

"What the fuck you bussing traps on our set for?"

"Man, aint nobody bust traps on ya'll set. That was ma personal. No matter where I'm at he buy coke from me," dude said and began walking away.

Caleaf stole (punched) him from the back and knocked him out. His manz took off running and Caleaf began stumping dude face in. Dude was younger and smaller than Caleaf, but he didn't care. To him every street dude was a grown man.

****

Caleaf ran Atlantic with an iron fist. It was a plus and a minus. Dudes who they had trapping out there didn't mess up money out of fear of what might happen to them, but Caleaf was young and his reaction to things sometimes brought heat to the block.

Later that night after Caleaf had knocked dude out, he was down the street at Niyumi's. Niyumi was a woman who converted her front pouch into a store. She sold a bunch of junk out of there. A car pulled over on Norris. Caleaf didn't pay it any mind. He got his stuff and began walking back to the set. The passenger got out of the car and crept right up on him. Caleaf was strapped, but never had a chance to pull it. The head shot dropped Caleaf. More came as he laid lifeless on the ground.

****

Shon was crushed when he found out what had happened to his cousin.

"It had to be the dude who he stumped out," Luck, who was another one of their trappers said.

"Do you know who he is," Shon asked?

"Yeah, not his name but he from Norris and Chase."

Shon and Luck rode all over town looking for dude but couldn't find him.

"He either in hiding, recuperating, or both. Caleaf beat him bad, that's why I know somebody else had to be with him. He could barely see when Caleaf was done with him.

"Do you know where he lives?"

"Nah, but I always see him at the Chinese store. We going to catch him, he always around.

****

The block got hot, and Roy ended up shutting it down. The police kept running down catching dudes with drugs, but through Roy's connects he was making the charges disappear.

"We're going to find out who killed him bro, cool out. You have to let stuff like that come to you. You don't want to do something dumb and get cased up," Roy told Shon.

Shon lit the Black and Mild and started smoking. It relieved some stress, but he wanted revenge.

****

Caleaf's funeral fell on a rainy Wednesday. The rain made everything seem sadder. Roy didn't let what happen slow him down a bit, but Shon did. Probably because he had to deal with his family, seeing his mom, aunt and the little ones cry.

Shon pulled up to the Chinese store on Chase. "Let me get a box of Milds," he told the Chinese man. It was a few dudes out there trapping. The ladies were out there too. Polock had the hood ratest. They seen him go into the store and began walking towards it like a bunch of penguins. Cee Cee was the first to come in. She was looking horrible, with some black tights, a white ting top and a black bonnet. She had a stuffy though.

"Hey Shon, you shinning," she said.

"What's up Cee Cee?"

He couldn't even lie and give a compliment back. She probably wouldn't believe him anyway.

"What you about to get into?"

"Nothing, why, you trying to come with me?"

"Yeah."

Before Shon got into the car, he took another look at the dudes that was out there to see if it was something wrong with any of their faces. He took Cee

Cee to a crib they had on Atlantic. She sucked him off but he ain't want to fuck.

"What happened to O'boy face out there, it look like dudes did him dirty."

"Who Freak? Somebody whopped his ass. They was tripping over that last week."

Shon had threw that out there and she bit. He didn't even see anybody face messed up when he was out there. She didn't know that. She was always high off of some kind of weed, wet, or pills. After Shon got his rocks off he took her back.

"His face was way worse than that," Cee Cee said.

"Who you talking about?"

"Freak, there he go over there," she said as she got out of the car. "When the next time you going to come get me?"

"I ain't going to forget about you. I know where to find you," he told her. She agreed because she was always in that area somewhere.

Shon kept looking at Freak to remember his face. Freak and his dudes were looking at the car, but they didn't know Shon or that Caleaf was his cousin.

Shon went and put all black on. When he rode back through it was too many people out there. He figured one or two of them may have been strapped. He pulled on Norris and Everett Street and sat there watching them. O boy was a grown man, but he was some kind of little dude. He was still trapping hand to hand.

Shon watched Freak and one of his dudes jump in the car, he followed them. They pulled in front of Crown Fried Chicken on Mt. Ephraim. When Freak came out the first two shots hit him in the chest and stomach causing him to drop his food and hit the ground. Shon hit the other dude up too. Afterwards he ran back to his car.

The cops were right around the corner looking for someone on Thurman when they heard the shots. Bout time Shon got to his car and tried to peel out they were right there. They crashed into his car, pinning it against a parked car. The officers jumped out with their guns drawn on him. He threw his hands up surrendering before shots were fired. They dragged him out of the car and locked him up. He was caught red handed with the gun and was charged with murder and attempted murder.

****

Roy had got Mr. Gilbert to represent Shon. He was given bail and was bailed right out.

"I told you to let that shit come to you. You could have caught him anywhere, now look."

Everything was going good until this happened. Even though Roy wasn't really phased, that was his manz. He took care of a lot of things for Roy.

"I know man, I fucked up. I acted off of emotions," Shon responded to Roy.

"Don't sweat it though, you going to be alright. I got people in places, trust me."

Shon heard what he was saying, but he was really thinking about how bad he messed up and how he was about to go away for a long time. Especially after getting caught red handed. That was almost unheard of. In his mind there was no way he was going to be able to beat that case.

Roy seen how down in spirits his manz was, so he took him over Philly to a strip club to cheer him up. Despite his manz catching a case he was good. Nobody knew yet but Roy had bought this big old warehouse on Haddon near Ferry train station. He had got it fixed up and it was ready for opening. For the last month he had been advertising it on Power 99, but as of yet no one knew it was his.

Chapter 13

When the time came for the club to open it was packed with a line stretched down and around the block. The first hundred ladies got in free. It was packed to capacity, both floors. There were metal detectors at the door, security throughout the place and Roy also hired off duty officers to patrol outside of the club. He knew how Camden dudes were and he didn't want anything going down. From his office he could see everything that went on in and outside of the club.

It seemed like the whole tristate was there. A lot of dudes Roy sold weight to and chicks he done ran through. Daniel was there along with all her friends. She usually wasn't allowed to go to clubs, but it was his and it was the grand opening. He caught her brushing a few dudes off who was trying to push up or dance.

The first day was a blast but he knew it wasn't going to be like that all the time, unless he got real inventive. Roy was feeling the business world. In so many ways it was like the coke game. His name was already popping because he sold weight, now it was really out there. That only brought him more weight sells and fed his ego to the point that he went and copped a Bentley. It was white on white with white 24-inch rims. When he pulled up in front of the club all eyes were on him. He got out and walked by everyone in line, kindly speaking to the people he knew.

"Is that Roy right there," he heard one of the ladies in line ask her friend?

Roy heard them but never turned around to look their way. It was another packed night. He went straight upstairs to his office.

"There goes the boss man right there Greg."

"Where," Greg asked after taking another sip of his beer?

"Right there, going up the steps," William said pointing with his eyes instead of his fingers.

Greg started observing Roy. "He don't look the part at all. We going to have fun with him."

"We can't sleep on him. He might not be as sweat as he looks."

They sat there drinking their beers the whole while keeping an eye on Roy's office. A couple of people went up there, mainly people like security and the club manager. Roy stayed for a couple of hours but left before the club closed. He was about to get on 676 highway when an unmarked car put its sirens on. He had no idea the car behind him was an unmarked car.

He pulled over on a street where there wasn't any houses. There was only cars riding by and bums at the corner. He didn't have anything on him, so he wasn't worried about going to jail. He looked through the rearview mirror and became a little worried. For a second he was worried that they weren't really cops but guys out to rob him. They had street dudes' swag and they had on regular clothes.

Greg walked to the driver's window and tapped it twice with his knuckles. "Roll the window down," he commanded tugging on the badge that was hanging on a chain around his neck.

"How may I help you officer?"

"It looks like in many ways playboy, you around here driving in this Bentley."

"Excuse me but….." Roy said trying to be polite until he was cut off.

"Excuse me but nothing mothafucka. I'm doing the talking, just listen."

Officer Greg's aggression was intimidating to say the least. Mainly because Roy was on this dark street and wasn't anybody else around. Officer Greg also had the look to go with his roar. He definitely had Roy's attention. Roy kept quiet and listened while he talked.

"Word is you're that dude. Well, I'm that dude you going to pay to remain that dude. I only let this be known once. Ten thousand every two weeks. Bring it to the laundry mat out Fairview near Chrestbury at 9:00pm. Starting on the 14th. You got it? I shouldn't have to tell you what's going to happened if you don't show."

Roy was looking at Officer's Greg's badge number, he couldn't get over the fact that they were actually trying to extort him. Then it had came to him, these were The Doom Squad. The undercovers he'd been hearing about who had been extorting dudes for years. They only extorted dudes who were really getting money. It was legendary how they were on it. Roy remembered a couple stories he heard of about dudes who didn't pay. They came like straight bullies and didn't offer any services in return. It was all about take with them.

Roy had got a good look at their faces, but from what he heard it was more than just two of them. When they got finish pushing up on Roy they jumped in their car and sped off. Roy sat there for a minute and took everything in. After a minute or so he put his car in drive and slowly drove off.

A lot of things was running through Roy's mind. His pride wasn't going to let him fold to them that easy. He automatically began going through his options. He could get them bodied, but they were cops, and he didn't know how many of them it actually was, or even what the others looked like. They could be any members of the force. He thought about not paying them, but he heard that they were serious guys. On the other hand, he figured if he did pay them then he was on some sucka stuff, that they might really start pushing their weight around. He had a couple weeks to figure it out.

He pulled into his driveway and was relieved from the pressure of Camden where he had to constantly be on point because he never knew what was next. There was no sight of Daniel's car so he figured she must be over one of her relative houses. He went straight upstairs.

"Hi Roy," Shamera practically whispered.

"What up, you here watching Tierra?"

"Yup, I just put her to sleep."

Roy was talking to her while walking to his room, she followed him. He was drained with a lot on his mind, so he wasn't really beat. He sat on the bed and began taking off his clothes.

"Where Daniel at?"

"She told me she was going to her moms, but she probably out tricking, who cares. She asked me did I feel like babysitting, and you know I did, hoping to get some alone time with you."

While she was talking Roy had gotten under the covers and cut the TV on. Shamera sat on the bed and started seductively touching him. Once she seen that it was working, she came out of her clothes and got under the cover with him. He didn't even get a chance to put on a condom before she started riding him like she had her CDL's. Shamera was going hard making all kinds of noises.

"Oh yeah oh yeah, I'm coming, oh yeah."

Crack!

Daniel slammed one of the lamps right into Shamera's head, knocking her to the floor. Shamera was making so much noise that either of them heard her come in, but she heard them and came up the steps charging.

"Bitch, I let you in ma house and you fuck ma man. You nasty hoe." While Daniel was beating Shamera up, she was calling her all type of names. She was dragging her by the hair, getting her hits in with the other hand. "This is why you always wanting to watch my daughter, huh?"

Roy hurried to put on his clothes. He didn't know rather to break it up or run out. He never seen Daniel in action before. She was always laid back. When she looked at him it seemed like something out of a scary movie. Then she attacked him.

"I gave you my all and this is how you treat me? My friend, in our bed. You ain't shit, I hate you, I swear."

She swung them over head punches like the rain man. He tried catching her arm but every now and then one would land on his head.

"Chill chill, let me explain."

"Explain my ass, it's nothing you can tell me. I seen it with my own eyes."

Daniel had stopped swinging and started crying uncontrollably. She calmly walked over and picked her purse up and began digging around in it.

"I love you Daniel, I was stressing and she aahhhhhh....."

Roy didn't get to finish what he wanted to say. Daniel pulled out her stun gun and gave him 50,000 volts. He hit the ground and she stung him again. Shamera seen what she did to Roy and ran out of the room.

"Bitch you better run. I'm definitely going to get you."

Roy was balled up on the floor, still shaking from the aftershocks. Daniel had spit on him and kicked him in the back. She went in the room started packing some of her things, woke her daughter up and left.

When Roy got himself together Daniel and his daughter was gone. The room was a mess, he couldn't believe what had happened. He sat there smelling like burnt bacon. It was a lot of blood on the floor from Shamera's head. He figured that she had to be hurt pretty bad because Daniel hit her over the head hard. His thoughts were scrambling, he just laid there until he went to sleep.

Chapter 14

"Ms. Simmons just let me talk to her," Roy pleaded with Daniel's mother.

Roy knew he messed up big. Women like Daniel was hard to come by. His house didn't feel like a home without her or their baby there. Couldn't no hoodrat he was hitting fill their space. It wasn't the fact he cheated because he was in the streets all day and she never said anything. It was how it happened, and who it happened with. Before he never realized how deep his feeling went for Daniel, but now he did. He knew that he loved her but now he was missing her.

"Give her some time Roy. She's hurt right now. Let her heal," Daniel's mother told Roy.

"When am I going to get a chance to see my baby? She can't keep her from me."

"Look, let me talk to Daniel. Come back tomorrow and you'll be able to take Tierra with you for a couple days or whatever, ok?"

"Alright," Roy reluctantly agreed and started walking away with his head down. He got in his car and sadly rolled away.

Daniel's mother played the peace maker. She was the only reason he was able to get his daughter. Daniel still wouldn't see him. Whenever he would bring their daughter back Daniel wouldn't come out. Either her mom or someone else from the family would come to the door. After almost a month and a half he had to face the fact that it was over between them. All the money he had wouldn't bring her back to him.

Roy eventually got over Daniel and got his head back into the game. The life he lived required him to be mentally present at all times. One wrong slip could cost him everything he worked so hard for.

The only other inconvenience was that dudes from Chase Street had shot Atlantic up. They didn't hit anybody, just made the block hot.

Roy left his auto body shop and got in a White Malibu. When he was making moves, he like to get low in rented cars. He was at the light when a tinted up Black Charger pulled next to him. Roy glanced over, he couldn't see anyone through the tint. He wasn't really worried about whoever was in there, but he could feel them staring at him. They were on his left side. When the light turned green the driver in the charger floored it making a right crossing in front of him.

"Wack as hell," Roy said under his breath. In his mind it was some petty playas who didn't know any better.

Fifteen minutes later he was riding downtown on Spruce Street when he was cut off by the same car. This time the passenger got out with a gun in his hand. Roy quickly put his car in reverse. Doing so he crashed into another car that had trapped him in. Three dudes from the first car were now out, two got out from the back car. All five started shooting his car up. Roy got as low as he could get in the car. He still felt a couple bullets rip through his body. He started to think it was over, he felt like this was how it was going to end. He started to feel himself fading out of consciousness. He tried to fight it but was no match.

When Roy woke up all he could see was fuzzy white lights. He was on the gurney with the doctors rushing him into the emergency room. That was the last thing he saw before passing back out. The doctors performed surgery and saved his life. Timing was critical, it helped that he wasn't far from the hospital when the shooting occurred.

The next time Roy woke up his mother, grandmother, daughter and Daniel was there. He could hear them talking to him and felt his grandmother holding his hand, but he was too weak and tired to respond. His eyes were heavy, he kept going back to sleep. He was in bad condition. The doctor had told his family that he was lucky to be alive.

Once Roy got a little stronger, he was able to go to rehab and therapy to get his body in good form. He had lost a lot of weight and that wasn't a good thing because he was already skinny. Now he was extra frail.

The ladies in his life kept visiting him, even Daniel. One day when it was just her and their daughter visiting him, he had broke down to her. He was laying down but sitting up. Their daughter was on the bed talking and playing with him. Daniel was sitting in the chair next to the bed.

"Daddy Daddy, when you coming home," his daughter asked?

"I don't know baby."

Their daughter was only two, but she was doing all the talking she could do. Majority of the time Daniel sat quiet unless Roy said something to her or when she said something to their daughter. At times he wondered why she came up if she wasn't going to say anything, but he was happy to see her and his daughter.

"Daniel, I'm sorry about what happened," Roy said looking Daniel in the face.

She knew what he was talking about. She nodded her head but didn't respond.

"I know I took you for granted. I didn't realize the woman I had in you until you was gone. Ever since then I been kicking myself in the ass, now look at me." Roy couldn't hold it any longer, he began tearing up.

"Daddy, you crying, why you crying," Tierra asked in her little precious voice? "Don't cry," she said and whipped a tear from under his right eye.

"I appreciate you being here. It means a lot to me."

Daniel held in her own tears. She nodded her head at everything he said."

"You can't give me the silent treatment forever, when you going to start talking to me again?"

"I don't have anything to say Roy. You left me speechless."

"Do you still love me?"

"I wouldn't be here if I didn't."

"Do you ever see yourself forgiving me?"

"I don't know, you really hurt me."

Persuasive Contracts | TyeMease

They sat there and had a heart to heart. It became clear to Roy the damage he'd done. For her to have a conversation with him was a step in the right direction. It was his hopes that they'll get back together. He figured with time that he'll get her back.

Roy was awakened by someone shaking his leg. When he opened his eyes, it was officer Greg dressed in all black. He had his badge hanging out of his shirt.

"Wake up weak back. You stink too, they gotta come change you. What's that a diaper or a shit bag you got up under there," Greg asked trying to lift the sheet up? Roy brought his hand down on the cover stopping him. Feeling vulnerable Roy was nervous. Greg had two partners with him watching Roy with the stone face. Either of them Roy ever seen before.

"I been keeping tabs on you and you're coming along pretty good. I'm happy for you, cause the sooner you get out of here the sooner you could start paying me my money," Greg said with seriousness.

To Roy these weren't cops. Nothing about them said cops but their badges. They were gangstas, thugs, worse than the dudes that he ran with on the streets.

"You got me, you understand what I'm saying?"

Roy didn't say anything. He kept looking in Greg's eyes as if he was searching for something.

"You're looking at me like I'm stupid. It's important that we get an understanding or you going to be under and I'm going to be standing. Believe me, you won't be so lucky next time. I'll see to it."

Roy was relieved once Greg and his two men left. The machine that was monitoring his heartbeats slowed down a little. He now knew who had shot him. Before Greg admitted it, he didn't know for sure. Roy never gave Greg trying to extort him too much weight, which caused him not pay him, which was the reason he ended up in the hospital. Now he seen that Greg was really about his.

Chapter 15

After more than three months in the hospital Roy was allowed to go home. He was about 75% of what he used to be. The physical therapy helped out a lot.

He went home to an empty house. His mom and grandmom would stop by. Daniel would send Tierra with them, but she never went over there. Even when he asked her to. Shon was one of the few dudes who were allowed to visit. He didn't deal with too many dudes to be letting them know where he lived. On the streets Shon held things down the best as he could. When he ran out of work, he started buying off of his manz from downtown. That was just until Roy came back.

"You ever find out who did it bro," Shon asked?

"Yeah, I know who did it. They paid me a visit while I was in the hospital."

"Who was bold enough to do that?"

"The Doom Squad."

Shon eyes brows raised up. "I heard about them. The detective dudes, right?"

Roy gave a little nod. "They been trying to push up on me."

"I don't even know what they look like."

"I didn't either until they came at me. I seen a few of them but I know it's more."

"What are they talking about?"

"They trying to get me to pay dues, ten thousand every two weeks."

"They bugging," Shon said.

"They got it for now. I'm going to fold because I can't move how I want, but I got something in store for them. You would think that after they hit me up, they would fall back. I didn't even know they had anything to do with it. They basically came in there and told me."

"I'm with whatever, I'll go to war with you if you need me."

"That wasn't even a question. I already know that, but these kinds of situations you have to be more strategic. Trust me, I got it. I'ma let you know."

****

Both of Roy's businesses were in good hands. His managers knew the businesses better than him, so they were still thriving. A lot of people were coming by the shop and club acquiring about him. Everyone heard what happened. At first it was talks that he wasn't going to make it, so for him to pull through was big.

Garnett walked in the shop and asked the cashier about Roy. The cashier looked at Garnett with a hint of fear in his eyes, but that was just because of the person Garnett was. He knew Garnett wasn't on any other stuff. He seen him come in there plenty of times and heard Roy talk well of him.

"Hold up, I'll go get him for you."

Roy came out of the back happy to see him. "What's good with you," he asked excited?

"What's good with you? Better yet, who did it? Just point me in the right direction and I'ma go. It hurt me when I heard what happened to you," Garnett was saying as they embraced.

"I know, I'm good now though. They can't stop me."

"You know who did it?"

"Nah, I'm still trying to put the pieces together," Roy lied.

"I haven't heard anything either. I been doing my own investigation. You know you ma guy."

"Yeah, I know," Roy said. For many reasons he didn't want to tell Garnett it was the Doom Squad. He didn't want Garnett to think that he was soft, he didn't want it getting back to the Doom Squad that he was running his mouth, and he wanted to handle things how he was going to handle them, on his time.

"Here go that money I owe you," Garnett said giving Roy fifty thousand wrapped up in rubber bands. "When the next time you going to have something?"

"I'm in the process of making something happen now.

Chapter 16

A couple days later Tuco came down from New York to pay Roy a visit. He offered the services of some of his soldiers if he needed. Roy told him that he'll let him know if he did, then they got to talking about business.

In no time Roy was back in the mix, networking. His flow never left. They were waiting for him because what he had was always right for good prices. They just were dealing with whoever they were dealing with while he was out of commission.

Roy was in his Bentley when he seen Vic's Benz parked outside of T.I.'s barbershop. He pulled behind it, and went in. Vic was getting his hair cut by T.I.. He looked like he'd seen a ghost when he seen Roy. Everybody in there spoke their peace and was congratulating Roy. He was a hood celeb, Vic was too. He was that dude until Roy walked in there and out shined him. Even his car out front out shined his. That Bentley made that 560 S Class look like a E 300.

Whatever conversations Vic was having with the fellas before Roy got there was now on mute. Roy's appointment was with Ruff. He sat in the chair getting his haircut, talking to the fellas, while watching the game like he never had gotten hit up. Him and Vic never spoke. They knew of each other but didn't really know each other like that, so there weren't any words spoken.

Ever since Roy got out of the hospital Vic weight sells had declined, so Vic was feeling some kind of way. He left the barbershop not feeling as big as he did when he walked in. Especially when he seen how bossy Roy's car sat up next to his. The first thing he did when he pulled off was call Greg.

"What's up," Greg said answering his phone?

"It's Vic, I just seen Roy. He back on too."

"How you know?"

"I just seen him talking business, plus some of the dudes who was dealing with me while he was down are back dealing with him now."

"Alright, thanks for letting me know. Still bring me ma money tomorrow on time. Don't have me come looking for you."

"I know I know, I got you."

Vic had been paying punk dues for some time now. In the process of hating on Roy he had sicked the Doom Squad on him because he didn't want to be the only one. He put them on a few other guys too.

Chapter 17

Roy was in the club handling business as usual when he noticed this beautiful young lady on the floor dancing. She had grace in her movements. He watched her for a minute to see if she was going to start throwing that ass around like all the other ladies in the club. Roy stood on the second floor looking down at her. They caught eye contact, then she turned away smiling. He knew he had her after that.

The whole night he kept his eyes on her. He seen guys trying to push up giving her their numbers, buying her drinks and trying to get her to dance with them. She always seemed uninterested but polite, accepting their numbers and drinks only to throw their numbers in the trash can that was next to the bar. She only got up to dance when her favorite songs came on. She danced but with no one particular.

Roy was never apprehensive about approaching a woman. He was feeling himself and he had reasons to. He figured that she had to have heard about him. After all it was his club.

Roy assumed that she wasn't from the city because he never seen her before. She looked young, but it was no doubt that she was a grown woman. He knew a grown woman from a girl who was underage. He wasn't one who was going to be fooled no matter how thick she was for her age. When she sat back at the bar Roy went downstairs and sat next to her.

"How you doing tonight?"

"I'm alright and yourself?"

"I'm wonderful now that you asked. I seen you scare a couple guys off. I didn't know what to expect."

"They were wack, I don't entertain wack dudes."

"I feel that."

"You don't remember me, do you," she asked?

Roy began examining her from head to toe, at the same time looking through his memory bank for the answer to her question. He shook his head no.

"I figure you wouldn't. We were in the 7th and 8th grade together," Maquita said as if Roy was supposed to remember then. "It's alright, I wasn't one of the popular girls anyway."

"Nah, I just don't be remembering much, especially anybody from school. Let me get your number so we can get reacquainted. Maybe you could refresh my memory."

She recited her number as Roy put it in his phone.

"Who did you come here with? You need a ride?"

"I'm by myself, but no I don't need a ride. Just don't forget my number," she said seductively smiling.

Roy smirked back and assured her that he wouldn't. Afterwards he went back to work.

"Marquita Marquita," Roy repeated in a low tone while going through the paperwork on his desk. "How could I forget a chick that look as good as her," he asked himself? He couldn't find that answer either. That night he was having sex with a different woman but couldn't stop thinking about Marquita.

A couple of days later Roy came out of his auto body shop and seen Greg on his phone leaning up against his Bentley as if it was his.

"I'll call you back," Greg told the person on the other end of the phone once he seen Roy coming.

"Ma man ma man, you always looking like money. This thing right here though," he said referring to the Bentley. "Just turns me on so I can only imagine what it does for the ladies. Come on, get in," Greg said inviting Roy into his own car.

Once Roy unlocked the doors, Greg got into the passenger seat. Roy was feeling like a duck. Greg had a thing for popping up at the oddest times. This time he was by himself, or at least Roy didn't see any of his manz.

"I see you back in business. Here go the address, date, and time that I need that. This shit could be real easy if you put ya pride to the side. You out here getting all this money, ten thousand is really nothing to you. Look at it like this, I got a family I have to feed too, so let me eat with you," Greg said smiling as he let himself out.

He still was smiling as he got in his car which was right behind Roy's. Roy peeped him through his rearview mirror. All Roy could think about was the saying, more money more problems.

When the day came to pay Greg, Roy was there on time with the money. After what they did to him, he wasn't messing around, he knew Greg would get his but until then he had to play the game. This time Greg wanted him to bring the money to a pizza store out East Camden.

Chapter 18

For Roy and Marquita's first date he invited her to go food shopping with him. She kindly accepted, even though she found it funny. Roy's fridge was empty. Ever since Daniel left, he had been eating a bunch of unhealthy fast food. His house had started to look like a college dorm room with all the pizza boxes and KFC boxes laying around. He had cleaned up before he invited her over.

"You got a nice house," Marquita complimented looking around. "Do you live here by yourself?"

"Yup."

"I can tell," she said after seeing all the dishes piled up in the sink.

Roy had bought about three hundred dollars in food. Marquita helped him put it all up, then volunteered to do the dishes while Roy did his best at cooking them something to eat.

"I hope you know what you're doing," Marquita said messing with him.

"Don't let this skinny stuff fool you," Roy said bluffing like he be cooking on the regular. He made a Spanish dish that his grand mom used to make. Some rice beans with chunks of meat in it.

"That was delicious, I'm stuffed," Marquita said once finished.

"I'm horny," Roy responded jokingly. They both laughed.

"I gotta use the bathroom," Marquita stated as she got up.

She came back downstairs with her shoes in hand. Roy was on the couch watching TV. He left the dishes on the table. Marquita sat on the couch next to him and started flirting, then they started kissing. They both came out of their clothes, the next thing he had her legs in the air as they were getting it in.

****

Garnett came out of the court room upset. The prosecutor had offered him a 12 year with a 6 year minimum, but he didn't take it. His lawyer asked him what kind of plea would he be willing to take? Garnett told him a 6 with a 3, his lawyer took that to the prosecutor, but she said that was ridiculous. Garnett told his lawyer to tell her fuck her. His lawyer tried to talk to him and told him that he might could get him a 10 with a 5 but Garnett wasn't trying to hear it, he just left.

The prosecutor didn't want to go to trial. Camden County hated to spend money, so he knew that they'll come down. He didn't want to go back to prison. He was tired of doing bids, he'd been jailing since he was a juvenile. 12 wit a 6 was a setback, he wasn't trying to hear that.

"Where the fuck is this bitch at," Garnett said to himself when he got in the house. Fee's car wasn't there. It was about 11 o'clock in the morning, he was wondering where could she possible be. She didn't tell him that she was going anywhere, and she didn't have to work. All he knew was that she better have a good explanation. He kept calling her, but she wasn't picking up. Then his calls started going straight to voicemail. He called her mother and sister's house, but they didn't know where she was at. Wherever she was she had their daughter and he had a feeling that she was up to no good. He tried to brush that feeling off, so he went back outside. When he came back in at night, he was drunk. It was around 10:30 at night, yet she still wasn't home.

Fifteen minutes later Garnett heard Fee come in the house. Garnett had jumped in the bed and pretended to be sleep. Seeing his car there was unexpected, Fee was used to him being in the streets all day and night. Fee took her daughter in the room then went in her own room. Garnett was pretending to be sleep so Fee was trying not to wake him. She tried her best to quietly take off her clothes. She got her clothes off and tried to get in bed, but before she could Garnett jumped out of bed with this big belt in hand. One of them heavy leather ones that hurt. Fee had her back to him when he got up.

Wap! Garnett slashed her across the back.

"Bitch, where you been all day," Garnett asked in the most serious voice?

On the first slash Fee flew across the room knocking stuff off the dresser. Garnett slashed her about five more times while talking to her.

"Bitch, you think you slick. You got ma daughter out all hours at night."

"Wait wait, please," Fee begged.

She was on the ground with her hands up trying to stop him.

"Get up, take ya panties off," Garnett told her. He grabbed her panties and smelt them to see if he could tell if she been fucked. "Lay down and open ya legs bitch."

Garnet got on his knees between her legs and started smelling her pussy. She was smelling like Dove soap, that's how he knew that she had been fucking.

"Where was you at?"

"I was out with my friends."

"Why you ain't answer your phone?" Garnett looked at her in disgust. WAP WAP! Don't ever leave this house again without letting me know where you going. Ya nasty ass is going to sleep on the floor tonight too. He didn't beat Fee how he usually did. It was times when she had to wear shades because she had raccoon eyes. She knew that she got off easy. That night she slept on the floor next to the king size bed that Garnett enjoyed comfortably by his lonesome.

The next morning he woke up and seen her thick ass laying there looking sexy. Messing with a dude like Garnett was a duty. Maybe she liked getting treated like shit, or maybe she didn't but what else made her stick around.

Chapter 19

"How is that court case coming along," Game asked Garnett?

"They on some bullshit. They came at me with a 12 with a 6. I can't take that. I'ma play the waiting game to see how low they'll go."

"How about Duke, what's up with him?"

"They gave him a 6 with a 3. That's what I'm trying to get but my record. That's his first charge, plus they knew none of that stuff was his."

"I got another connect too. Dude Vic be having them," Game said.

"Is his prices better than Roy's," Garnett asked?

"He said for me he'll give them up for 30, but he soft as cotton so you know."

"Yeah, I know." Without saying it they both understood each other.

The first move Game made with Vic he copped five bricks of coke. Not all of it was his. Him and his dudes always went in together because the more they bought the better the numbers they could get them for. Garnett snatched up one for himself. He was still dealing with Roy too. Everything that came from Vic was good so Game started dealing with him on the regular. Eventually it was only right that Garnett dealt with the man with the lower prices as well. He started falling back from Roy and so did some of Roy's other clientele whom Vic had begun serving.

"You ready for me," Roy asked Garnett?

"I'm good right now, but I'll let you know when."

"Come by the shop so I could talk to you."

Roy had a fresh shipment and was trying to get rid of it as fast as it had came, but he was running into some stumbling blocks.

About an hour later Garnett showed up at the shop.

"What's good bro," Garnett asked as they shook hands?

"I gotta ask you a question. I have to know because it's been a minute."

"What's up?"

"Who you copping from now?"

"Nah man, you on some bullshit," Garnett said laughing.

"I ain't on no bullshit. I'm trying to figure out who fucking up ma flow. A lot of people talking about they're good now, like it's something better for the low around."

"You really wonna know?"

"Hell yeah."

"Dude Vic, ma manz put me on him."

"I know who you talking about. What's his prices?"

"Ma manz got him giving it to us for 28."

"Alright, I'll match that."

"So you could have been giving me them for that price all along."

"Not really, I have to profit too. You know how it go. When you done with that bullshit he sold you come see me."

Garnett didn't leave Roy's shop with a good feeling. He could tell that Roy was on some b.s.. He had become known for using his power to get people killed. Garnett wanted to make sure he got to Vic before Roy did. He got up with Game later that day.

"You ready to get at O'boy," Garnett asked Game?

"Vic," Game asked?

Garnett nodded his head yeah.

"We only been dealing with him for like a month."

"I'm saying anything could happen with dudes like him. You know how it is, here today gone tomorrow. He can catch an indictment and we'll miss out on all that cash."

Garnett didn't want to tell Game about Roy. He wasn't all the way sure, plus Game might a had his own plan to mess up Roy's plan.

Garnett and Game began following Vic around, peeping the houses he went to and the ladies he dealt with. Each time they followed him in different cars. He didn't move around like a boss at all, which made it easy for them. If the Feds was on him, they'll have an open and shut case.

They knew what houses was his stash houses because he went to them every time before he met a drop. Two weeks of following him and they had his patterns down. One day they followed him to Chester PA to a mall parking lot where he met some dude. When he got in dude's car he had a bag, but when he got back into his car, he had two different bags. They figured that had to be the connect.

"You see that bro," Game called Garnett and asked?

They were in two different cars watching.

"Yeah, I'm on it. What's up with the other dude. That's money in them bags."

"He probably lives out here somewhere."

"Look bro, the money in them bags, I'm following him. Stay on Vic."

Garnett didn't care where they were at. He wanted everything and he knew there was at least a couple hundred in that bag. The part of Chester PA they were in was like the suburbs. He followed dude to the next town over. Dude pulled into a garage and Garnett slow rolled by, got the address and kept moving. He used his GPS to find his way back to Camden.

Mean while Game was on Vic. When they got to Camden Vic went to what they already knew was one of his stash houses in the Fairview section. Game pulled over about a block from the house then called Garnett.

"Hello."

"What's goodie," Game asked?

"I'm on my way back now. How is it looking on your end?"

"He went in the house with them thangs."

"Alright, play him close," Garnett said before hanging up.

Vic didn't stay in the house long. Within fifteen minutes he was in and out. Game didn't feel a need to continue to follow Vic. He kept an eye on the house until Garnett arrived.

"This might be easier than we thought," Game told Garnett when he got in the car.

"Why you say that?"

"Because them bags are in the house and he left."

"How long has he been gone?"

"About forty five minutes. Since the last time we talked."

"Lets go break in there then," Garnett said.

They didn't know that it would be so easy, yet they didn't mind either. They got in through a side entrance and went upstairs. They were quietly trashing everything, going from room to room finding money and guns but not what they were looking for. Garnett walked through the hallway, looked up and seen an attic door. He pulled the string that was hanging, and a ladder begun coming down, and he went up there.

The attic was small, Garnett couldn't stand up straight. It was dusty and dirty up there. Besides that, it wasn't much up there but children's toys. Right near them he spotted the bags that he was looking for. He grabbed them and headed back down the ladder.

"I know you heard me calling you. Come on, he just parked his car," Game said whispering and rushing Garnett.

"Oh shit, where we going to go."

"Come on, in here," Game said grabbing one of the bags out of Garnett hand.

"Hold up, let me close the attic," Garnett said trying to go back, but Game wouldn't let him. They heard Vic put his key in the door.

"Fuck that attic bro, it's wrecked. He going to know somebody was in here regardless."

They went in the middle room and hid in the closet. When Vic opened the door, his heart dropped. Everything was tossed around, his first thoughts, hopes, and wishes were that they didn't find them bricks of coke. He slammed the door, pulled out his gun and ran upstairs where he saw the attic ladder pulled down. In his heart he knew it was over. He went up there and seen that everything was gone. He came out of the attic going from room to room like a mad man. Even he didn't know what he was looking for. When he got to the middle room Game and Garnett could see him out of the closet door. It had a horizontal screen. They had their burners out behind the clothes that were hanging up. If Vic would have opened that door it would have meant death for him, but he didn't. He went through the rest of the house. A half hour later they could still hear him in the house cursing and talking to himself, making phone calls. Once he left, they got out of there through the back door.

They didn't tell any of their other manz about that caper. It was unexpected, they had intentions of at least bringing along their manz JB to be the driver, but sometimes when opportunity knocks you have to answer or you 'll lose out.

"This a nice come up, we ain't telling nobody about this one," Game said.

"Ain't no need to. I wonna celebrate after this come up though. I might take ma chick somewhere special. What you think," Garnett asked looking at Game to see what he was going to say?

They had twenty bricks of coke sitting on the table. Ten in front of each of them. The total amount of money was 68,500, which they split. That was basically a bonus.

They treated that mission like it was any other mission they had pulled off, regular. They had been doing this since they were young. As they'd gotten older their capers had gotten bigger, but easier because it was the same routine. They were always on go.

That night Garnet went home and had sex with Fee. The next morning he woke her up wanting to take her and their daughter somewhere special but Fee didn't want to go anywhere with him, so he just went to the hood.

Chapter 20

Roy and Marquita had went to Dave & Busters in Philly to play the games. It was a way for them to let their inner kid come out and see each other open up. It was Marquita's idea. They had been dealing with each other for about four months strong now. Roy was feeling her. She wasn't Daniel, but Daniel never gave him a second chance, so he kept it moving. Marquita was more outgoing and spontaneous.

After they left Dave & Busters they went back to Jersey and mellowed out at the AMC movie theater in Deptford. The whole time while watching the movie Marquita was hugged up on him.

"Am I your lady Roy," Marquita lifted her head off of his chest and asked?

"Why you ask that?"

"I would like to know where we stand so my feelings won't get hurt."

"Yeah, you ma lady," Roy said assuring her. He didn't want to keep talking about it because he was into the movie.

It seemed like Marquita was secure with that answer. She cuddle back up to him and resumed enjoying the movie.

****

Gervonta Davis had a fight coming up Saturday. Roy made a few calls trying to see who was going to fly out to Las Vegas with him. So far it was only him, Shon and Jeff. After making his calls nobody else seemed interested. That wasn't a surprise, he was always talking about how dudes be getting money and don't be doing nothing but the same stuff. To him it was like, why you getting money in the streets if you going to be doing the same things dudes who ain't getting money doing.

That Thursday night they flew out to Las Vegas and checked into the MGM Grand. They had booked a high roller suite. Shon and Jeff put their stuff in the suite and went back out to gamble. They didn't even tell Roy they had left. He was stuck looking at this brochure some guy handed him on the street. It had a bunch of pretty escorts in there. Roy was trying to figure out which one he wanted.

Roy's phone began to ring. He dug in his back pocket pulling it out. "Hello," he answered?

"Yo, we about to go gamble. You coming," Shon asked?

"I'll be right there," Roy told him. Gambling was something he liked to do, even though he was horrible at it. He didn't mind losing a couple of dollars though.

They were at the Roulette table talking slick, feeling themselves, betting on every number they felt they had luck on. All of them were up, even Roy. Out of nowhere these three young ladies were standing next to them like they were with them the whole time. It was two white girls and a black girl. Roy noticed them before placing his numbers. He looked at them wondering where the hell did they come from, but he knew that he was in Vegas.

The ladies were real giggly, cheering them on and rubbing their bodies against theirs. Everything was extra, from the way they jumped up and down to make their breast bounce every time the fellas won, to how they held their arms when they lost.

"Come on, I need some of ya good luck, blow on these," Jeff said getting one of the girls to blow on his chips before placing them on his numbers. When he won the white girl began jumping up and down as if she won. Her breast was about to jump out of her shirt. The old heads around the table were just looking waiting for them puppies to pop out.

"You coming with us tonight," Jeff asked one of the chicks?

He looked over at Roy with a smirk. Jeff already knew she was with it by the way she was in his face. They only had a couple nights out there, but while there they planned on acting a fool.

They went from playing Roulette, to playing craps, then to blackjack. All the while the chicks tagged along. Eventually they agreed to ditch the chicks and head to a couple other places. Jeff wasn't feeling that. While they were out, he was trying to pick up every prostitute he seen.

"Dam bro, you gotta pull up on that one. I'm paying for that. I don't give a fuck what you say."

This prostitute had on a blue skirt with a short jean jacket with some six inch heels on. She had track star legs with a fake Sarena Williams butt that looked lopsided.

"You bugging, I ain't pulling over," Roy said.

"Alright, let me out then," Jeff said.

"I'm really about to let you out so you can do all the tricking you want." Roy pulled up on the prostitute and began slow rolling along side of her while she walked, giving Jeff a chance to talk.

"Yo baby girl, you working," Jeff yelled from the passenger with his head out the window. Roy kept looking trying to see her face. As they got close enough, she turned around with the extra strong tight face.

"Who you talking to, me," the transvestite said in the most feminine voice he could muster up? It was still deep though.

"Oh shit," Jeff said surprised. He quickly put his face back in the car and straightened up. He was embarrassed.

Roy and Shon began laughing at him.

"That's a dude," Shon said smacking Roy on the shoulder and laughing at Jeff.

"You still wonna get your freak ass out. You know what goes on in Vegas stays in Vegas," Roy said laughing.

"Man pull off," Jeff demanded. Jeff was heated. They kept clowning him with little jokes through out the whole night.

It was a line outside of the club. They pulled over and went in. They really didn't pay too much attention to the people who were in line. Vegas had all kinds of people coming there. They assumed that they were tourist like them. Once inside they realized how out of pocket they were. It was all white people in there, most had mohawks with shave sides. The males and females both wore eyeliner, leather pants and jackets with chains hooked to their pants. The techno music was booming. Shon and Jeff was acting up dancing. People were looking at them like they were crazy. They didn't stay there for long. After a couple drinks they left. Around the corner there was a hip hop club. More of their speed, with people of all ethnicities. Every chick they pushed up on was from somewhere different. They stayed there for a couple hours.

While walking back through the casino they seen the same chicks they had earlier posted up with some white old head dudes who were gambling. They had their own chicks with them that they had bagged out of the club. When they got to the suite the chicks who they had bagged from the club were acting like they never seen the inside of a hotel suite before.

"Are ya'll some type of ball player," the white girl asked?

The new girls they picked up were white, black, and Asian.

"He plays for the Eagles," Roy lied talking about Shon since he was the biggest. The dipsy bunny got excited. "And he's a rapper. I'm their manager," Roy claimed.

"If you watch football you'll see me," Shon said and took off his shirt.

That's all the ladies needed to see to be convinced. They all wanted a piece of him, but he chose the black girl. They sat on the couch.

"I watch rap videos, how come I never seen you," the curious white girl asked?

"Bring ya ass over here. Why you asking so many questions," Roy asked her? "How old are you?"

"I'm twenty," she said.

"That's why you asking all these questions. You a young girl."

"I'm a grown woman."

"Yeah, we'll I'ma treat you like a grown woman, come on."

Roy took her in the room, and both began undressing. She began kissing on him. Once she seen his manhood, she became a little hesitant.

"Let me go to the bathroom," she said looking down at his erection.

"Hold up, come here," he played feeling on her butt.

"Wait, I'll be back," she said giggling.

She made her way to the bathroom, and he chased them little cheeks. She ran in the bathroom and shut the door on him. Jeff was ripping the little Asian chick in the corner. Shon was getting head. The white girl peeked out of the bathroom, when she seen the coast was clear from Roy she tried to run back to where the bed was, but Roy caught her from the back.

"Why you playing games. You get off playing games, don't you?" Roy had her hugged up from the back. She turned around and wrapped her arms around his neck.

"Yup, I do. Feel how wet I am." They were hugged up face to face. Roy reached around and felt her pussy from the back. That thing was soaking wet. Roy walked her over to the big window where they were looking down on the city. He bent her over and started hitting it from the back. She was a noise maker. Out of all the ladies she was the loudest. Roy was in it raw. He was trying to dog her, but she was loving it. After he came, she turned around and begun sucking him. He was all the way soft. She was trying to get him back rocked up so she could continue getting hit. The little chick that was running in the beginning was now showing how much of a freak she really was. Roy stood there looking out of the big window at the city, the bright lights, cars and people. All he thought about was how good life was.

Jeff was done trashing the Asian chick. She was laying on the floor still shaking with her fingers in her mouth.

"Let me get some of this," Jeff said walking up on Roy and the white girl.

"Go ahead," Roy said. He backed out of the chick mouth and went over to Shon's chick, the black girl. She was the only one of them who had a fat ass. She was bent over the couch sucking Shon. Roy went behind her and slid right in, messing her rhythm up. As Roy stroked her, she moaned while she kept topping Shon off, adding a harmonic vibration to her head game that Shon was loving.

The Asian chick came over and the black chick stop sucking Shon and the Asian chick jumped right on him. The whole night they were getting it in, switching and swapping DNA.

Roy was the first to get up in the morning. His stomach was growling and bubbling. He ordered breakfast for everyone then went to the bathroom. When he came out everyone was awake.

"Room service ain't come yet," he asked looking at Jeff?

"Nah, I ain't hear anything. I just woke up."

All three of the chicks were sitting close to each other. When Roy walked by they began giggling.

"What ya'll laughing at. I know I'm getting a little gut. All rich mothafuckas got guts. That mean we

146

eating," Roy said. Then he walked past Shon and Shon started laughing too.

"That ain't why they laughing, you still got tissue stuck to you."

Roy looked back and seen that he had a few squares of tissue still stuck between his yaks.

"Oh shit," he said and went back to the bathroom.

"Do a good job this time," the white girl shouted to him laughing.

Shon tipped room service when it came. The original bill was on Roy's credit card. Roy came out of the bathroom in time. They had a little breakfast feast. Afterwards they got the girls to clean up and got them out of there.

Later that day Roy went down to the pool area to chill. He had his swimming trunks on with a towel around his neck, but he didn't plan on getting in the water. Shon had some chick on his shoulders. Him, Jeff, a couple dudes and all these chicks was playing ball in the pool. It was a rooftop pool. Roy sat on the lawn chair next to some chick who was laying on her stomach sun tanning. The sun was glistening off of her sunscreen cheeks. He took out his phone and called home, but nobody answered. He had been getting the answering machine since he left. His mind couldn't help but to wonder. What if the feds ran down on his crib, what if she (Marquita) robbed his house. He quickly got rid of them thoughts, but it was other thoughts. What if something happened to her or if she was out there being a whore. All these what ifs was messing with him.

"Roy, what's good bro. You ain't beat," Jeff asked trying to get him in the pool with them?

"Nah, I'm going to go get a massage," Roy said as he got up.

"Yo, make sure you tell the lady that's giving you the massage that you want a deep tissue deluxe," Jeff suggested from his own experience.

****

Roy had this little pretty masseuse. Blonde hair, blue eyes, petite body, look like she could have been one of Donald Trump's secretaries. Everybody knew he only kept pretty bunnies around him. Roy had asked for the deep tissue massage not even knowing what it consisted of. The room was dark, the candles were lit, natures music of the sea played low in the background. Roy was enjoying the back massage as she hit every spot that needed it. He kept going to sleep and waking up. About a half an hour later she told him to turn over. She began massaging his chest and shoulders, then undid his towel. His manz stood up and his eyes popped open. She started massaging his manz then started sucking it. This was something he didn't even request, yet he was stuck looking at her thinking, *fuck it, if this is what she want to do.*

"Thank you, but what was that for," he asked after she came back from spitting his babies out?

"You ordered the deep tissue deluxe, that's what you got. That'll be $150," she said smiling.

Roy got back up with the fellas, they went and got something to eat then went to the Floyd Mayweather's Boxing Gym. Floyd had a fleet of Rolls Royces out front. Roy couldn't keep his eyes off of them.

"I gotta get me one of them," Roy said.

"I think that's the Ghostbuster," Jeff said. He didn't really know his cars like that.

Roy didn't like the old Rose Royce models, but he loved the new body ones. He didn't think any car was messing with them. They were too bossy. He knew if he came through in one of them that he'll shut the whole city down.

In the gym there was a bunch of Floyd's fighters training. A bunch of other people around watching. Jeff picked up some gloves and began hitting the heavy bag. His jabs were popping, making noises. He was hitting the bag hard and fast. Everyone's attention turned to him. Once Jeff notices how much attention he was drawling he took the gloves off. One Spanish old head who was in Floyd's camp had made his way over to Jeff and started asking him questions.

"Where you from youngen?"

"I'm from Camden New Jersey."

"You box?"

"I grew up boxing, but you know I had got into the streets."

"You're sharp, you should start back. How much do you weigh?"

"Like 175lbs."

"How old are you, 25?"

"Nah, 23."

"You should really consider getting back into the game," old head suggested. It'll change your life." He took Jeff over to introduce him to a couple other guys.

"I ain't know you was into boxing like that," Roy said once they got back into the car.

"That's ma thing. I can't play basketball for shit, but I can box. Ma uncle use to have me in the gym when I was younger."

"What was they talking about over there?"

"Asking me questions, seeing if I wanted to train with them."

"What did you say?"

"I told them that I'm not from out here."

"That don't mean nothing," Roy said. "I should leave you out here man. You got a gift, you supposed to nurture that and put it to use instead of wasting ya time in the hood, feel me? The goal is to get rich, if you good at that you going to get rich. Especially with them backing you. You know how they coming. Trust me you rather be in the ring than risking ya life and freedom in the hood messing with them dirty chicks. You gotta think past that. Everybody in the streets is losers bro. I don't care what we got or how much we're getting because we always are going to end up dead or in prison. Even the chicks that deal with us. They know that one day their child is going to be without a father. That's when they're going to move right on to the next man, who is going to also be a street dude. Probably ya manz from the next part of town."

The whole time Roy was talking he was giving himself a reality check too. That's when he realized that he was getting tired of the game. It had become boring. He had more fun in spots like Vegas then in the hood, but like most dudes he didn't have enough power to let power go. Jeff and Shon sat there listening. They basically did the same things they did yesterday for the rest of their days there, gamble, party, and at the end of the night take some chicks back to the hotel suite. What else was it to do in Las Vegas?

The next night at the fight the stars were out. Gervanta Davis punished his opponent in six rounds. Back in the car Roy called home and Marquita picked up.

"Hello,"

"Where you been at?"

"I was at my mom's house. I didn't want to be here by myself," she said.

"Are you good?"

"I'm fine, when are you coming home?"

"Real soon."

They talked for a little while longer until Roy pulled up to the after party. All type of chicks were out there. The after party didn't end until the morning, a few hours before they had to catch their flight.

****

In mid flight the flight attendant who was pushing the cart with the snacks and beverages stopped by Roy and Jeff's seats and asked them would they like anything. They both grabbed something to eat and drink off of the cart and she kept it pushing.

"I need you to handle something for me when we get back," Roy told Jeff while unwrapping his Snicker Bar.

"You mean someone," Jeff asked?

"Yeah."

"Who?"

"This dude Vic. He in the way."

"I know who you talking about," Jeff said.

"I'ma give you twenty stacks as soon as we get back."

Chapter 21

After Vic's house had gotten robbed, he was running around like a chicken with his head cut off. He had his peoples doing investigations on the streets trying to find out what they could. Camden is small so it's not hard to find out what you wonna know. If you could keep ya business on the low in that city, then you was good. Vic didn't know it but after his bricks had got stolen his connect had got robbed too.

Garnett and Game had brought JB along for that one. They didn't tell him about the other caper they pulled off on Vic, it wasn't a need to.

"You sure we ain't lost," Game asked Garnett. "This the second time we rode down this block."

"Nah, I got this. It's around here somewhere, I know what the block look like."

It was late night, and they were in the car with all black on in the suburbs of PA, a commonwealth state. Game felt like they were riding around in circles. Garnett turned left and realized that he was on the street.

"Here we go right here," he said. He pulled to the end of the block. "Me and Game are going in. Get in the driver seat and keep this thing running. Keep me on speed dial in case something happen, like the cops pull up or something," Garnett told JB.

"Got you bro," JB responded.

They got out of the car and started walking down the quiet street. JB cut the car lights out and slouched down in the seat. When they got to the house Garnett knocked on the door. After a few knocks this older lady answered. Garnett pointed the gun at her face and held one finger to his lips indicating for her to be silent. She didn't say anything but looked like she had an accident in her panties. He pushed her inside then put his mask on. Game had already had his on. Garnett didn't care if she seen him. He didn't have any plans on getting caught. He just didn't want the dude to see him.

Game had brought an old head man downstairs. Garnett knew that wasn't the dude he followed.

"Go search the rest of the house," Garnett told Game. "Basement and everything."

Game sat old head next to his wife. He started cuddling her, trying to let her know that everything was going to be alright, because she had begun crying as Garnett held them at gun point.

"Who else is in this mothafucka?"

"Nobody else is in here sir," the old head answered.

"Where's the dude I followed here the other day?"

"You're talking about our son. He don't live here."

Game came back in the room where Garnett was. "Nobody else is in here, don't tell me we're in the wrong spot."

"Nah, o'boy is their son. He don't live here though."

"Dam," Game said disappointed.

"I don't care what they say about where he lives, that money in here because I ain't see him leave with it. So, either we leave with that money or I'm killing somebody."

Garnett sounded like he meant business. The lady started crying even more.

"Look, if it's money ya'll want I can get that for you."

"Alright, lets go then," Garnett said. Old head got up and started leading the way. "Watch her dog, don't have no mercy on her either. That crying shit don't work with me."

Old head took Garnett upstairs to his bedroom. Garnett kept the gun pointed at the back of his head incase he tried something stupid. Old head went in his drawer and pulled out a few stacks. It was hard for Garnett to tell how much it was, but it wasn't enough.

"Mothafucka you think I'm going through all this to waste my time? Do this look like a toy gun in ma hand? Give me this shit," Garnett said snatching the money. "Now where the money ya son brought in here yesterday?"

"Oh, that money," old head said stupidly recognizing that he could have gotten smoked for the dumb move he just tried.

"Yeah, that money. I'm starting to think that you want me to shoot ya old ass."

Old head took him to another room to a closet. Garnett recognized the bag. He grabbed it, seen that it was money in it, searched a couple different spots to make sure he wasn't missing anything. After seeing that there wasn't anything else he took old head back downstairs, they tied them up and they left.

"What took ya'll so long," JB asked as he pulled off?

Chapter 22

When Roy came home Marquita was up expecting him. When he came through the door, she ran up hugging and kissing him like he was a soldier who had just came back from a tour and she was happy that he came back alive.

"I miss you baby, did you have fun?"

"Yeah, I had fun." Roy was tired because he didn't really get any sleep on the plane.

"Did you bring me anything?"

"I brought you me."

157

She was talking about something material, but she didn't say anything. She just smiled.

"I need some money so I can go shopping. I seen this Prada...."

"What happened to that money I left right here on the dresser," Roy asked pointing to the dresser where the money was.

"I spent it," Marquita said.

"What you spend twenty five stacks on?"

"Clothes," she responded.

"You should be good then. That was only three days ago. Ain't that much shopping in the world."

Marquita was a shopaholic. Only wearing high price name brand clothes, but all on Roy's expense. When he told her she should be good she tried to act like she wasn't mad, but he could tell that she was.

Roy took a nap and was awaken by Marquita bringing him his phone.

"It's your lawyer, I forgot to tell you that he called earlier."

"Hello."

"Mr. Mckennie, we're having a gathering tonight and you're invited," Mr. Gilbert said.

"Alright, no problem, I'll be there," Roy responded.

Roy was thinking, *of course he was invited, he was the coke guy, the plug, their go to guy.* He knew as long as he had them on his hip the streets were his, and since everything has a price, that was a price he was willing to pay. He got up, took care of everything he had to take care of early, then later he went to the gathering.

****

Ever since Jeff feet had touch down he had been hunting. Only if he went as hard at boxing as he did in the streets it would be no doubt that he could become champion. When it came to the streets it's like he zoned out and gave it his all.

It took days for him to catch up to Vic. He had spotted his car and knew that he had to be nearby. He pulled over and waited for a sighting. That's when he seen him near the laundry mat. The sun was setting, but where Vic was at it was lit up by the store lights. Jeff got out of the car and started walking. He crossed the street to get on the same side as Vic. Vic seen him coming but didn't pay him any mind. Jeff acted like he was about to walk by, but as soon as he got close enough, he pulled out and started shooting Vic. Vic hit the ground and Jeff emptied the clip on him.

Chapter 23

Roy and Marquita had just came back from New York. Marquita went shopping like it was Christmas, but the only person she got stuff for was herself. They both had bags in their hands going in the house. Marquita had so many that she had to go back to the car and get the rest of hers. Only two of the eight bags were Roy's.

Marquita had Roy open with her hands in his pockets. She gave him good pussy, good head, and a good time. They stayed going out to different spots enjoying themselves. Shopping was her thing though. She ain't never have so much high fashion designer clothes until she ran into that money Roy was making.

"I'll be back baby," Marquita said giving Roy a kiss on the cheek before leaving the house.

She wasn't a house chick like Daniel was. She barely played the crib. She was always over her mom's, sister's, house or one of her girlfriend's houses in the city. At least that's what she always told Roy. Since they didn't live in Camden, he thought she wanted to be around her peoples. Staying in the house wasn't his thing either.

****

"It was a fight," Roy asked responding to his club manager over the phone? "Alright, I'll be there in a moment. Bout time Roy had got there it was police everywhere, somebody had gotten shot.

"Dudes came back and shot dude on the corner. The good thing was it wasn't on our property," Archie, the club manager said.

"Shut everything down. We don't need this kind of attention. Next thing you know they'll be trying to shut us down for good."

"Alright, I'ma take care of that right now."

Little by little people started spilling outside of the club. Roy was about to leave because he wasn't to beat for anybody but he didn't get a chance to go anywhere. This chick that he knew was at his car holding him up.

"Where you going Roy, can I come?" The liquor was heavy on her breath, it turned Roy off.

"I'm about to go handle something," Roy responded showing a lack of interest.

She was trying to convince him to take her, but he wasn't beat. She must couldn't read facial expressions. Then his passenger door opened, and Shamera got in.

"Hey," she said.

"Hey yaself," he responded not even saying anything about how she violated by just jumping in his ride. He rocked with her so she could get that, but he took a mental note to keep his doors locked because that could have been anybody. The other chick had left once he started talking to Shamera.

"Did you ever get back with ya girl after that day?"

"Nah, I had to get a new chick. Daniel don't even talk to me anymore. Have you talked to her?"

"No, I know she don't want to talk to me. What you about to get into tonight?"

"I'm chilling tonight, we could get up some other time though."

"Let me get a ride home then."

After taking Shamera home he cruised the city. Nobody was really out except a few dudes he spotted here and there trapping. He rode through his sets, but didn't stop. He couldn't be seen out there how he used to. He was getting too much money. Plus, he didn't know half of the dudes out there. They knew him though. Every so often he'll pop up with Shon and a few of them a be out there.

He had the most popular club in the city. That's where it seemed everyone was until he shut it down for the night. Even though things were going well he was getting tired of everything. Everyday stuff had become boring to him. He ain't mess with too many dudes. Shon was the only one he felt like he could really trust, and he was about to go to prison. Them thoughts reminded him that he had to work his connection so Shon could make out alright in that situation he had got himself in. Roy was so beat that he went home and took it down early.

The next morning Roy called his Lawyer and told him he was coming to see him. When he got there Mr. Gilbert's secretary was all smiles when she seen Roy. The two people who was waiting to go into Mr. Gilbert's office was looking at her. They knew either she liked him, or they had something going on already.

"Mr. Gilbert, Mr. Mckennie is here to see you," she said through the phone on her desk.

"Tell him I could wait until he takes care of these good ladies out here," Roy said.

Amy repeated what he said, and Mr. Gilbert said alright. Roy set there for another twenty minutes talking and flirting with Amy. In between her answering the phone and doing paperwork she was laughing at everything Roy said like he was the funniest man in the world. The two ladies came out and Mr. Gilbert buzzed Amy.

"You can send Mr. Mckennie in now."

Roy walked in there, they shook hands and embraced like Mr. Gilbert was a brother. Roy helped himself to a seat. Meanwhile Mr. Gilbert went to his mini bar and grabbed a bottle of D'usse and poured the two of them something to drink.

"I don't plan on staying for long."

"Why not," Mr. Gilbert asked. "I don't have anymore appointments until after lunch." Then he pulled out his lunch bag. "My wife packs my lunch now. She has me on this healthy diet, so I have to sneak a snack in every now and then. So, tell me, what's the problem?"

"I just wanted to know what was going on with my brother Tyshon's case?"

"Oh, he's going to be fine. Me and the prosecutor was talking about him the other day. You met Todd, haven't you?"

"Yeah, we met."

"He's the one handling the case and that's my guy."

"What kind of time will he have to do?"

"We'll, he's going to have to do some time, but I'm going to make sure it's under ten years. Is that alright Mr. Gilbert asked looking at Roy for approval?"

"Try to get it closer to five."

"I'ma see what I can do."

****

Later that day Roy took his daughter and Marquita to his grandmom's house for dinner. His mother and her dude were there along with other family members. Roy's mom Keisha should have had a camcorder and a microphone because she was interviewing the heck out of Marquita, asking her all kinds of questions. She wasn't being ignorant, neither was Marquita when she was answering her. Roy's grandmom was her sweat self towards Marquita. Keisha had a reason why she was asking the questions she was asking. Marquita reminded her of herself when she was younger. The way she looked and dressed. Keisha wasn't fooled by the innocent role she was playing in front of them.

When it was time to leave, Tierra didn't want to go. She wanted to stay over her great grandmom house. She called her mom mom.

****

The next day Roy had got a call from his mother. She went straight to talking about Marquita.

"I don't know about that new girl you got. What's her name, Marquita," she asked answering her own question?

"Come on now mom," Roy said.

"You my son and I know a good woman from one who is not. I don't trust her, be careful baby. What happened to that good girl you had?"

"We broke up."

"Boy you don't know when you got something good. You have to treat women according to how they act. The ones that be out all day, partying and clubbing, they not to be brought home to the family."

Roy heard what she was saying but he nixed it. Marquita was his girl. The little time they were together was more than the time him and his mother ever spent together.

CHAPTER 24

Roy picked Shon up from his house to fill him in on what his lawyer told him.

"I talked to the Lawyer earlier, we trying to get you something around five years."

"Yeah, that's what's up, I'll definitely take that," Shon said feeling better. That sounded way better than the twenty and thirties he knew guys was getting. Plus, he basically got caught red handed. He didn't know if Roy really had it like that, but at the moment it sounded good.

"He said that you're going to have to do some time, but believe me you in good hands. Told you I got you bro. Who you got that's ready to take your spot? It has to be somebody reliable and trustworthy. You know them dudes better than me."

"I got a couple dudes. I been out here breeding these dudes. I'm going to put ma manz on though."

"Alright, just make sure he can handle the responsibilities."

****

When Christmas came around Roy bought Tierra two big trash bags of toys but didn't get a chance to see her open any of them. He dropped them off at Daniel's mother house. He made sure every gift had from daddy on there. To drop the gifts off was the only time they let him in that house. When he spoke to Daniel, she hit him with the head nod and her mom escorted him back outside. He also bought Marquita a Black Jaguar as a Christmas gift.

****

Roy and Garnett met at the shop to handle their business. Roy noticed that Garnett had like a smirk on his face. Not like a sneaky smirk, but one as if he had something on his mind or knew something.

"What's up with you, why you keep smirking," Roy asked?

"Because you got some shit with you," Garnett responded.

"Why you say that," Roy asked curiously. He had a feeling he knew what Garnett was referring to.

"You know what I'm talking about. I know you was going to do it though, I knew it."

Roy began smiling. It was understood without being said that they were talking about Vic getting killed. Garnett didn't tell him that he came up off of Vic before that. He left with ten bricks. That was more than he usually bought from Roy. His squad was turning it up. They opened a set downtown and it didn't take long for it to start banging. He took Game and JB their work and went about his business. He always made sure his trappers had work on the block.

The prosecutor and Garnett's Lawyer thought that he was going to trail for the case he had pending. He was due to pick his jury on Monday. Garnett left the house early Saturday morning, he returned around two in the afternoon. It wasn't like him to come home until late night. He played the streets all day. He came home early to put some money up and get something out of his daughter's room. He grabbed a water out of the fridge then headed upstairs. He was about to go to his daughter's room when he heard noises coming from his bedroom. He knew Fee was home because her car was outside. He knew them noises all to well and the only time she made them was when he was in her. He opened the room door and what he seen next seem like a nightmare. No real dude would ever think that it would happen to him. (Not Garnett, he gets too much money and put too much work in them streets. Don't they know this Garnett bitch, don't he know he fucking with death. Even worse, don't she know better than to disrespect especially in his house on his thousand dollar mattress.)

Garnett pulled out his gun. Dude was pounding Fee from the side holding her leg up. They had no idea Garnett was there. He walked right up on them.

"O shit," dude said jumping out of the pussy. "Yo, I'm sorry bro, I ain't know she had a man," he said trying to cop a plea. Garnet wasn't really paying him any mind.

"Get ya shit and get out before I end ya life," he told dude.

Forget trying to put anything on, dude collected what he could and got out of there. Fee was cuffing the covers like she was trying to hide her nakedness.

Garnett was furious, his nostrils were flaring, he had yet to say anything to her which really scared her. She started crying then got up.

"I'm sorry Garnett," she said. When she got up the covers slowly fell revealing everything she was just giving to another man. As soon she got close to him, he put the barrel of the gun to her stomach and pulled the trigger. She hit the ground cringing. He got her phone, dialed 911, put the phone on the ground near her mouth then left. He didn't want her to die, just wanted her to hurt.

Fee was trying her best to talk to the operator. It didn't take long before the cops came. Someone else had heard the shot and reported it. Fee was taken to the hospital where she remained for a couple of days. The detectives came there trying to question her, but she didn't tell on Garnett. They still wanted to question him.

Garnett was supposed to pick his jury that Monday. He didn't even bother to show up to court. In his mind he was a wanted man, but he really wasn't until he had missed that court day. A warrant was issued, and they ran down in his crib a couple days later. Since he was already in hiding, they didn't catch him, but it made the area where he was from hot.

CHAPTER 25

Roy heard about Garnett's situation. He knew he had charges pending. Now he thought he was on the run for shooting his girl too. Roy was at the A.M/ P.M when Greg pulled up on him with two of his men. They were ice grilling Roy like he did something wrong. Roy kind of feared these dudes, but because he was paying his dues, he figured he was good.

"What's happening with you," Roy asked?

Greg was as hood as any hood dude, it's just he had a license to kill which made him even more dangerous. He got out of his car and entered the car with Roy.

"Word is you got ma manz killed," Greg said.

"What the fuck is you talking about," Roy asked?

"Watch ya mouth when you talking to me." Greg made it his business to make it known that he was the alfa male. Roy's weight and height made him look like a little boy around Greg. He didn't bother to respond when Greg told him to watch his mouth around him.

"Word is you got Vic murdered. Now you got to pay his dues. So, double that for me when we meet up."

Roy was looking at him while he was talking, thinking how Greg must really think that he was sweet. Greg got out of the car and slammed the door. It was messing with Roy that Greg even knew, he was wondering how. The streets had a way of finding out everything, no matter if a person had a mask on or if wasn't anybody there. *The streets must literally talk,* he thought. Greg had his size 13 on Roy's neck and Roy was fed up. Still when that day came, he doubled up on that payment.

After making a few weight sells Roy got up with Shon. He had the young boy who Roy was supposed to meet with him. Roy seen him out there before but didn't really know him. He was always so busy he never really got a chance to socialize with his trappers. It was like how many of Walmart employees met the owner, none probably.

"Roy meet Dame, Dame meet Roy," Shon said formally introducing the two. Shon sat in the passenger and Dame sat in the back.

"I heard a lot about you Dame," Roy said.

They had went over Philly to hang out. Roy wanted to get to know Dame, get a feel for the kind of guy he really was. He trusted Shon's judgment, but still everything needed his stamp of approval. Dame was only 17, but in the street that's a grown man. Roy knew a couple chicks who he was related to. Roy didn't question all crazy, they just talked about everything. What was expected, the duties, and how nobody outside of them was supposed to know where anything was.

More importantly than anything Roy needed to feel Dame's vibe. If that wasn't there it was no way he was going to trust him.

Later that night Roy had got a call from Garnett. He thought he had skipped town, but he was on schedule to re-up.

"What you thought you wasn't going to hear from me, this thing don't stop," Garnett said.

Roy dropped Shon and Dame off and went to meet up with Garnett.

Garnett only copped a brick this time. He wasn't sure when he might get snatched up, so he had to make sure his money was there when he needed it. Everything on the streets he planned on counting as a lost. He knew how dudes on the streets were when they thought it was over for someone.

"I see you been in the cut," Roy said.

"Yeah, they gotta catch me this time. Everything is going to be what it is until then."

"Why you don't get out of here, move somewhere else?"

"That shit overrated, I be out all night, just sleep during the day."

Garnett wasn't the only one from the city who thought like that. It was a lot of dudes who was wanted still in that little city. Some of them been on the run for years.

Roy nodded his head as though he understood. Really his mind went to capitalizing off of the situation. "You still doing contracts, right?"

"Of course, I'm always working. You need me?"

"Yeah."

"Who is it?"

"You heard of the Doom Squad?"

"The Vice dudes, right?"

To Garnett the Doom Squad was a myth. He knew nothing about them other than what he heard from other people because they didn't go at guys like him. They only went after guys who they thought wasn't going to kick up.

"That's them, they been trying to come at me but I ain't trying to bow down," Roy lied trying to make it seem as if they just started pushing up on him.

"They still the police you know that right?"

"I know, if you don't want to do it don't worry about it."

"Nah look, just pay them a couple of times to get them comfortable then we'll make it happen, because they might be a little cautious since it's going to be ya first time."

Garnett was hesitant, but for the right price even the cops could get it, especially crooked ones.

"Alright, let me know," Roy said.

That wasn't something he could just ask anyone to do, so if Garnett wasn't willing to do it, he was going to leave it as that.

CHAPTER 26

Roy woke up and got out of bed. Marquita was still sleep. He Went downstairs, as he walked through the house, he became furious. He couldn't help but to think that Daniel would have never had his house looking like it was. The house would have been clean, and he would have been waking up to some breakfast. He was having a moment which had him thinking about what his mom had told him about good women being hard to find.

"Wake up," Roy said shaking Marquita.

"Whaaat, why you waking me up," she whined?

"Get ya lazy ass up so I can show you. It's 11 o'clock, you should have been up."

It took her another five minutes to get out of bed. Roy was fed up. It was all on his face. Marquita had no idea what was going on. After she got herself together, he began walking her through the house.

"What do you see," he asked?

"I don't know, what do you want me to see," she asked sounding irritated?

"I want you to see how dirty this mothafucka is. Look at them dishes piled up. You don't have no job, at least you could do is keep the fucking house clean and cook."

Marquita sucked her teeth and ran some water so she could start the dishes.

"Clean the rest of the house too," Roy said before leaving the kitchen. He went out and bought some breakfast. Something he never did when Daniel was living with him. He was gone for a couple hours. When he came back the house was feeling clean and smelling fresh. *It's a shame you have to make a chick clean nowadays,* he thought to himself.

Marquita was in the bathroom scrubbing behind the toilet when he went upstairs. When she got up, she had beads of sweat on her forehead.

"I'm sorry baby, I was slipping. It won't happen again," she said and kissed him on the mouth."

"It's alright, clean yaself up."

It was football Sunday. Roy went and sat in front of the TV to enjoy himself. After Marquita got out of the shower, she came downstairs in the usual she wore around the house, almost nothing. She was looking and smelling good. Roy noticed, but he wasn't paying her any mind. Marquita sat next to him and began unzipping his pants. Once she got his manz out she started giving him his just due. *Right on time*, Roy thought because it was half time. Bout time half time was over she had topped him off well, swallowed everything and let him finish watching the game in peace. *What more could one ask for*, Roy thought to himself.

****

A couple dudes was posted up down the street from Roy's set on Atlantic and Norris. Dame was running the block. He seen fiends buying drugs from them but instead of going down there to confront them he called Shon and waited for him.

"They been down there all day bro. I ain't want to do anything stupid, so I just waited for you. Whatever you want to do I'm with it," Dame said.

Shon looked down the street and seen about six dudes. Local nobodies who he'd been seeing around. These dudes weren't knee deep in the game so they didn't know how real it could get. They were looking back up the street like they knew Dame and Shon were talking about them.

Shon ain't want to do anything that was going to make the block hot or jeopardize him catching another charge on top of the one he already got. Mr. Gilbert had gotten him a 7 with an 85%. He had to do about five years. He let what was going on ride for that night.

The next day when Roy came through, they were back out there. Roy wasn't one for open confrontation, and even though Shon was, Roy made him fall back because he was about to go in to do his time.

"I'll get them out of here. Just keep doing what you been doing."

They ended up being out there for a few days because Roy couldn't get in touch with who he wanted to get in touch with. Garnett didn't have a stable number so Roy had to wait for him to get in touch with him first. When they got together Roy told him the deal.

"Dam dog, you stay wanting somebody killed," Garnett said.

"Mothafuckas is habitual line crossers. You know how this game is."

"I don't be having them type of problems. Dudes know I play so they stay out of my way."

"I got a whole one for you."

"Say no more."

They got in the car and Roy rode through the block so Garnett could see who they were.

"Them, that's a piece of cake. Garnett knew that they were nothing like the dudes he was used to going up against. Not only were they out of pocket and off point. They were sitting there smoking and drinking as if they weren't in violation. Garnett had let Roy know that that'll be taking care of asap.

Garnett only paid for one of the bricks, the other was given to him for the hit. Instead of Garnett putting the work in himself he subsidized it to Randy for five stacks. Randy knew where one of the dudes stayed at.

Randy didn't waste any time, he went to the dude house he knew and knocked on his door with his gun in his hand. Out of everybody who was in the house dude answered the door and Randy started hitting him up. He emptied the clip on him, then ran off.

The guy who got killed friends disappeared off that corner after that. It was rare for a Camden murder to make the news but that one did. The family was on every news station crying, talking about how he was such a good man, that he never been in trouble with the law etc.…. They were putting pressure on the authorities to find his killer.

Roy was home watching the news when he seen dude face appear on the television. He nodded his head in approval. He didn't believe any of that innocent stuff his family was talking.

Word was going around that the wrong person had been killed, that it was supposed to be his brother. Shon told Roy the same thing. Roy seen him out there when him and Garnett rode through. Whatever was being said Roy didn't think much of it. As long as they were no longer out there trying to sell drugs, that's all that mattered.

CHAPTER 27

Tuco came down from New York. Roy was always trying to impress Tuco. He wanted to let him know that he was doing good. Plus, he knew that he was still in touch with Fernando and that Fernando would be proud of him.

Tuco was one of them no nonsense type of dudes. He spoke and moved with authority. When he came to town everything was on Roy. They went to the finest restaurants. They visited Ms. Rosa and Luci. Then they went downtown where they visited some more relatives. Tuco knocked on the door and a little old lady answered. The sight of Tuco brought a big smile to her face. They hugged then Tuco and Roy went in. Roy took a seat on the couch while Tuco chatted with his family.

The door opened and this big dude walked in. Everything about him said that he had just came home from prison. His weight was up, he had a ting top on with long braids to the back, and he was smoking a Black and Mild. Roy was the first person he seen when he walked through the door. They locked eyes and got stuck. They both looked familiar to one another, but either could put their finger on how or from where. The few seconds they were locked in trying to figure where and how they knew each other everything seemed to be going in slow motion, but it was only a few seconds.

"What's good," dude said breaking the awkwardness.

"What's going on," Roy replied?

Dude went in the kitchen where Tuco was.

"Oh shit, Uncle Tuco, look at you man."

"What's good nephew, when did you come home?"

"I been home for about four months now."

"Four months, and you still shinning? You must not be messing around," Tuco said knowing his nephew be sniffing dope. That's the reason why he never dealt with him on the money tip.

"I'm done with that unc, I can promise you that. I'm trying to get money now. I'm trying to get one of them Bentley's like you got out there. When I seen that thing parked outside of the house, I knew you had to be here."

"That's not mines, that's ma manz car out there."

"He got that off. Where ya manz from, he looks familiar?"

"He from Camden, I don't know what part. That was Fernando's guy."

"If that's ma brother's manz I know he good peoples."

"You going to put me on or what unc? I'm ready."

Tuco looked into his eyes to make sure he really meant what he said about leaving that smack alone. Eyes don't lie, that's why bullshitters could never look people straight in the eyes.

"I'm going to put you in with my manz out there. I got you. He going to make sure you good. I barely come through but I'm going to make sure he makes sure you good."

They walked back into the living room where Roy was. Tuco introduced the two of them.

"Roy, this is Rampage, Page this is Roy."

Roy stood up and him and Rampage shook hands. Roy still had that crazy feeling that he remembered Rampage from somewhere. He just couldn't figure out where. Rampage had that same feeling, but either of them said anything about it. Rampage usually remembered the faces of people he did something to, but he knew he couldn't have done anything to Roy because he was too young. He had just come home from a five year bid and didn't remember doing anything to any young boys when he was home before.

Tuco set it up for Roy to front Rampage something. Roy didn't have a problem with it. He knew if he messed anything up that Tuco had him covered. When they left Tuco had let him know that it was a strong possibility he would mess the money up, that if it happened not to sweat it. He just wanted to give his nephew a shot. Tuco didn't stay in Camden a whole day. He collected the two hundred thousand Roy owed him then went back up top.

The next day Roy dropped Rampage off a brick. This was the first time Rampage had ever had a whole brick that he didn't rob somebody for. Also the first time he had to really get money with it. He couldn't sell it for dirt cheap how he did when he would rob somebody for it. Roy didn't ask where he was getting money at or anything. He had Roy's number and he was to get at him when he was ready to re-up.

Later that day when Roy was out and about, he had got a call from Tuco. "Roy, I know you ain't do this on purpose, but whoever you got around your money you need to check them, because fifty of them stacks were missing a hundred dollars. Look like somebody was purposely peeling off a hundred."

Tuco knew all too well how it was trying to keep money around people. People were always going to try their hand, especially when it's a lot of money because they figure you couldn't or wouldn't account for it all.

It was hard for Roy to hear what he was hearing, but he believed him though. Tuco wasn't going to lie over a few dollars. Not when they were getting the kind of money they were getting together. As much as Roy didn't want to face it, he had to, Marquita had to be peeling him for his bread. She was the only one who had access to the money that he had just given Tuco. Either that or he miss counted and he didn't believe that it was the latter.

"Alright, I'ma get to the bottom of it and send you the money with what I owe you."

"No problem," Tuco said and hung up.

Instead of saying something to Marquita right away, Roy decided to set her up. He put some more money in the exact same spot. He counted it twice to make sure it was on point.

CHAPTER 28

Friday was sentencing day in Camden County. It was the day Shon had to go in to start doing his time. Dame was running both blocks. Shon had taught him a lot, but now Roy was schooling him to do things his way.

Early in the morning Marquita got up, took a shower, put on something nice then started fixing her hair and makeup. All the noise she was making eventually woke Roy up.

"Roy, I need some money baby."

"Dam, can I open ma eyes," he responded?

She was standing in front of the mirror checking herself out, making sure everything was good. Poking her lips out, making the fish face as she put on her makeup. Roy got up and brushed by her on his way to the bathroom. When he came out, she asked again.

"You can have that money right there," Roy said referring to the money on top of the dresser. It was about a three thousand dollars. Marquita had already counted it. She left the house soon after and headed to Camden. Roy had to cook his own breakfast, and the house was untidy again. Roy just looked around shaking his head. He looked at the time on his phone and seen that he had to go get his daughter soon.

****

Marquita pulled up on Utah street and went into this house. A short dark skin dude answered the door, and they gave each other a hug and kiss. He was gripping her butt. She had on some blue jeans with some six inch heels. When they got back in the house Marquita made herself at home taking off her shoes and going to the refrigerator. She made them something to eat.

"I brought you something," she said and put the money she had got from Roy on the table.

"Dude going to get you if you keep stealing from him," O boy said and grabbed the money.

"I ain't steal this time. He's actually generous. He just sweet, so I take his stuff. He has so much, he don't be knowing what's missing." Marquita went over and sat on Trev lap. "You miss me baby?"

"You already know," Trev said, and they kissed. "I'm home now, when you going to leave that lame?"

"Soon baby, soon," she said and gave him another kiss for insurance.

"I just don't want you falling in love with him."

"I'm not falling in love with him. You're the only man for me so stop worrying. All the money I be bringing you, I figure you'll be proud of me. When you were locked up you told me if I find a sucka, get what I can get out of him, don't let no man play me. I took heed. I found someone to take care of me while you were gone and I been stacking baby. I ain't show you the stash yet."

"I am proud of you, but I can't sit here like my pride ain't a little hurt. Especially knowing another man had his hands on you."

"He not getting any of this though." Marquita got off of his lap and on her knees. She unbuckled his pants and started giving him head. Trev sat his left hand on top of her head, closed his eyes and put his head back as he enjoyed her suck game.

The whole time Trev was locked up Marquita was sending him money on Roy's expense. She kept it a hundred with him about Roy. Trev knew that she was going to do her regardless so instead of sitting in prison stressing, wondering if and who she was in the world having sex with. He schooled her, and she respected it. As long as she sent that money, came to see him, and didn't get pregnant, he was good. She was his ride or die chick. The type of chick a lot of dudes who were locked up wish they had. A chick that was for her dude no matter what. He couldn't get rid of her if he tried, but then again why would he.

CHAPTER 29

It took Rampage about two weeks to move that brick. Way too long for Roy, but when he gave it to him he didn't count on it coming back how he did with everything else that he put on the streets. What he gave him was in a pot of its own. Still Roy messed with him about it. They conversed while they made their move. Both suppressing the feeling that each looked familiar. Roy contributing it to his lack of trust in dudes, especially grimy looking ones. Roy felt like he couldn't trust anyone since his manz had gotten locked up and his girl was stealing money from him. Rampage contributed his to him being nervous because of all the dirt he did.

****

Life on the run for Garnett wasn't as bad as he thought it would be. He liked creeping around the hood at odds hours of the night. It was like he was invisible. He knew everything that went on and nobody knew anything about him. The only thing he didn't like was that he had to be on point for cops and snitches. He tried not to let anyone see him whom he wasn't doing business with or a chick he wasn't dealing with. The mission Roy came to him with was still on the table. Usually, he would have done it by now, but this one he thought about so much that he kind of discouraged himself and forgot about it.

****

It didn't take long for Marquita to start going in Roy's Money stash again. When he went to check this time, it was obvious because he had set everything a certain way and as hard as she tried to put it back how she found it she couldn't. He didn't trip, he knew she had to come home, so he went about his regular day.

Marquita came home around 1:30 am. For any dude that was a direct violation. She didn't have a job, have to attend to anything, or didn't let him know that she was going anywhere particular. That was just her regular. She was a street runner.

Roy had been home a couple hours when he heard her come in. Still fully dressed, he went downstairs and smacked the shit out of her. (Smack)!

"You like stealing, what you thought I wasn't going to find out?"

189

She fell to the couch and held her face in awe. With her mouth open she looked at him like he was crazy. He stood over top of her like a mad man.

"Pussy don't be hitting me," she said as she force kicked him in the balls. He bent over in agony grabbing himself. He was trying to get the feeling out of his stomach. He couldn't even take a deep breath. She then punched him as hard as she could causing him to fall to the ground. The punch looked like it hurt, but he was still grabbing his balls. The pain from that was over riding everything else.

Marquita ran upstairs and started grabbing some of her things. When she came back downstairs Roy was waiting for her. He had recovered from the pain and was ready to whoop ass. As soon as she hit the bottom steps, he began going on her like she was a man. He hit her in the face a couple of times, but it was mainly body shots. After he beat her up, he kicked her out with anything.

Marquita called her cousins to come get her. They were deep, all girls outside of Roy's house being loud, calling Roy out, talking about how they were going to beat him down. Marquita's face was beat up. They were feeling some kind of way. One of the chicks had bust Roy's windows out. He still didn't come out. One of his neighbors called the cops. That's when they all left.

For Roy the relationship was over, but he received a call from Marquita a couple days later. He was annoyed by her voice. The crazy part was she was acting like everything was supposed to be forgiven.

"You still mad at me Roy?"

"What you think? You stole from me. I'm not going to be dealing with somebody who stole from me. I gave you whatever you asked for, why steal?"

Marquita didn't respond.

"See you can't even answer me that."

"I'm sorry Roy, can you forgive me?"

Within the couple of weeks Marquita had been feeling the effects of not having Roy in her life. She wasn't able to live the same lifestyle that she was able to when she was with him. When he kicked her out mostly everything he bought her was in the house with him.

"I doubt it," Roy responded.

"Can I have my stuff and my car back please," Marquita begged.

"Hell no! I Bet that's the only reason you called. You selfish and money hungry. You ain't getting shit. I paid for everything so I'm burning it. All ya jewelry is going to ma next chick," he said then ended the call.

****

Marquita had went to see Trev days later. Her face was still messed up but, not how it was after everything first happened. She wore some big shades and tried to cover half her face with the hair from her wig. As soon as Trev seen her, he knew something wasn't right.

"What happened to ya face," he asked?

As soon as he asked that question, she began crying.

"Roy did it, he beat me up. He found out that I was stealing and started punching on me like I was a man." She began hugging on Trev while sobbing telling him what happened.

"I told you that he was going to get you," Trev unsympathetically said. He knew if a chick would have stolen something from him that he would of did the same thing.

Marquita stopped crying and took her head off of his chest and said, "That's all you gotta say?"

"What you want me to say. I told you before it happened."

"It's not what I want you to say, it's what I want you to do."

"What you want me to do?"

They both took a seat on the couch. Marquita took her shades off and Trev's eyebrows raised as his eyes got big in shock. He found it funny and wanted to say Daaam, like smokey on the movie Friday when he saw Red's black eye. He knew that she wouldn't find the humor in it, so he kept his smile hidden under a concerned face.

"He has a lot of money in his house, and I know where all of it is. You're going to have to kill him because he going to know that it was me and he going to come looking for me. He might be a punk, but he's not stupid."

Trev thought about it. He thought about how them boys (cops) responded fast in the suburbs. Then parole had placed him on a curfew. That's all they had to do was get pulled over and he was done. That wasn't enough to keep him from risking it all though.

"How much you think he got in there," he asked?

"He keeps at least a few hundred thousand in there but it be in different places because he be having it for certain things."

"You sure it be that much in there," Trev asked? A few hundred thousand was enough to move any dude, especially a street dude. As soon as Marquita nodded her head Trev said, "alright, I'ma make it happen. I have to call ma dudes."

CHAPTER 30

"You hear that," Shamera asked?

Her and Roy was laying there after just having sex. The television was the only device on throughout the house. Roy looked at her wondering what she was talking about. "Nah," Roy said. He sat up trying to hear what she heard, but all he could hear was dogs barking. "I don't hear anything," he said laying back down.

Then he heard something, got up, put his boxers on and grabbed his burner. Shamera got up too.

"Give me a gun," she whispered.

Roy gave her a little 9mm. They both posted up near the door. Shamera was naked holding her gun up, looking like one of Charlie's Angles. One of the dudes came in the room with his gun out. He cut the light on and met Shamera's 9mm. Roy came from the other side with his gun on him.

"Put your gun down nice and slow," Shamera said in a low tone knowing that it was others in the house. Dude put his gun down, then his hands up. Roy picked the gun up. Shamera set dude down on the bed and held him at gun point.

Roy went out into the hall where he caught the other dude coming out of the back room. "Drop it or I'ma murder you," Roy said.

The look of disappointment struck dude face. He began laying the gun down real slow. The whole time keeping his eyes on Roy.

Shamera held her gun pointed at the other dude as he sat on the bed. She stood a little to the side of him, both hands gripping the pistol. For whatever reason her having him at gun point didn't frighten him at all. He took the time out to admire her body. Her brown skin was shining. She was every bit of 160lbs, thick without a stomach. He caught himself fantasizing for a minute.

Shamera seen how he was looking at her and she made a disgusted facial expressing. She had no idea what he was really thinking though. Her arms were getting tired of her holding the gun up and unconsciously she had gotten a little too close. Close enough that dude smacked her arm and tackled her to the ground.

The gun hit the floor. Dude didn't get a chance to see exactly where it went but she did. He jumped on top of her, and she started digging his eyes out. He hit the floor, grabbing his eyes, hollering in agony. She retrieved the gun and started shooting him.

****

Roy heard the tussling, but he couldn't let O boy out of his sight. Then came the shots. He was hoping that Shamera was the one doing the shooting. His hopes were confirmed when he looked down the hall and seen Shamera standing there.

Trev was downstairs panicking, he tried to find the stash spots Marquita had told him about. One of them was in the basement under the front porch. He was tucking the money in his bag when he heard some shots. He didn't even get all of the money. He quickly made his way back up the steps so they could get out of there. In his mind his dudes had killed Roy too soon and messed everything up. Once them shots were fired it became a race to get out of there before the cops came. He didn't know that his boys weren't the ones doing the killing.

Roy had heard someone else moving around in the house. He still had his gun on dude. He took a couple steps out of the room to look down the steps, that's when he seen Trev. Trev lifted his gun, and they started shooting at one another. Trev fell and got out of there. Roy didn't bother to chase him.

"What happened," Shamera asked rubbing the jaw dude she killed had got a punch in?

"Somebody else was downstairs," Roy said.

"I'ma go see if he still in here," Shamera said.

"What's up with the other dude?"

"He dead," she responded and went down the steps.

"Who sent you," Roy asked? Dude had scared all over his face. Things obviously didn't turn out how they expected. He seemed hesitant to speak so Roy took him in the room where his manz laid dead. "You see ya manz, do you want to end up like him?" Dude still didn't say anything, he just looked at his dead homie stuck. "What you deaf? I'm talking to you. I asked you a question. Now who sent you?"

"It was the chick Marquita you used to mess with. She messes with ma manz Trev. She said you had a lot of money in here, but she was only going to tell us if we agreed to kill you, which we did, and she told us about this mission.

"You didn't kill him yet," Shamera asked when she came back in the room. Give me the gun, I'll do it."

"Nah, I'll do it," Roy said.

"The other dude got away."

"Go put some clothes on and leave, I don't want you getting caught up in this. I know the cops are on their way."

Shamera did what she was told. Roy shot dude in the forehead. He knew it wasn't any self-defense laws in Jersey so no matter the circumstances he knew that he was going down. Bout time Shamera was ready to leave the house it was too late. The police had the house surrounded. They locked her and Roy up and charged them.

Roy bailed Shamera out. He had to sit because he violated his probation. When his lawyer came to see him, he was curious to know how he got himself into such a dilemma. Roy explained everything. His lawyer told him that everything was going to be alright. Roy knew that this situation was really going to test the power of his connections.

When they went in the courtroom the prosecutor was one who Roy haven't seen before. She was coming for his head. He knew the judge though. The judge was just going through the motions. The young prosecutor was feeling like she was on her A-game, making all type of arguments against why Roy shouldn't get bail. The judge denied Roy's bail because of his probation.

After the hearing Roy's lawyer told him that she was a new prosecutor trying to prove herself. The next hearing there was a different prosecutor. A guy whom Roy knew. Everything was in Roy's favor. Without going to trail the charges on Roy and Shamera were dropped. The judge ruled that it was self-defense being as though they were the ones clearly under attack. They didn't even get charged with the guns that were found with scratched off serial numbers on them. Roy's probation was reinstated, and he was home within two weeks. He felt like he had diplomatic immunity. The hood was shocked when they seen him come through. Everybody thought he was finished.

Roy celebrated with Shamera at a club. He didn't know she was that thorough. That night he seen another side of her. She responded better than a lot of dudes probably would have in a situation like that. For that he decided to keep her close. She wasn't just a good fuck anymore. She was an asset. Still, they ended their night between the sheets.

CHAPTER 31

Everything was back to business as usual for Roy. Now that he knew Marquita had sent her little manz to try to kill him, he had something in store for her. He couldn't stop thinking about that while he was in the county. He got up with Garnett and put him on everything. He gave him pictures of Marquita, her address and told him about the dude Trev. All the info he thought he needed Roy provided. He wanted her punished for what she did.

Roy went to New York to see Tuco. Tuco had heard about everything through Rampage. Roy explained how he beat the charges, and everything was back on.

During the day Roy played the auto body shop, at night the club. He had his manz Sam making all the weight drops for him. Sam was one of his workers at the auto body shop. Now he was doing more than fixing cars. With him doing that Roy was able to stay off of the radar.

Roy was looking down from the second floor of the club when he seen three big dudes making their way through the dancing people. Dude in the front looked up and Roy recognized Greg. They came up and went into Roy's office. Greg's two men posted up near the door. Greg shut the blinds. Roy's mood changed as their negative energy filled the room.

"Congratulations, I thought you was finished. You must really got an angel looking out for you. Greg waited for a response from Roy but didn't get one. Roy had that look on his face that basically said what do you want. He didn't have to pay him for a couple more days. Roy felt uncomfortable under the constant stair of Greg's men, but he made sure that he got a good look at them. He wanted to remember their faces.

"This is a nice office," Greg said sitting in Roy's chair. He started opening and closing drawers. Then he put his feet on his desk, then folded his hands on his stomach. Roy felt violated in every way. Nobody could image him getting pushed up on like this.

"You got the life right here my boy. I could see me getting involved with something like this. What you think?"

"It's not about what I think," Roy responded irritated.

"I think it is because I'm going to be your new partner. What do you think about that?"

"That's not going to happen. You're going a little too far with this shit now."

"What I tell you about ya mouth. You do a couple of weeks in the county, and you think you hard body now. Don't make me break you up." Greg got up on some old head stuff and got in Roy's face. He balled up his fist and put it near Roy's face. It was actually almost the same size as Roy's face. "I'ma excuse you because I know you might be feeling yourself after beating them murders. By the way, how did you beat them?" Roy just looked at him but didn't bother to answer. "Don't let me find out you snitching. You know I could find out stuff like that."

"I'ma give you a couple of weeks to make your mind up on that other thing. You better get a lawyer to drawl up a contract soon. I want 51%. Don't end up like last time, you might not be so lucky," Greg said before leaving the office. Greg and his squad went downstairs and started talking to some ladies. Roy opened the blinds and watched them.

"Come on, lets get out of here. He a bitch, I'ma take him for everything he got, little by little," Greg told his partners looking back up at Roy's office window.

The only way Roy could describe how he felt when Greg came around was as if he was stripped of his manhood. Garnett acted like he didn't want to get at them, so he thought about calling Jeff. The difference between Jeff and Garnett was that Jeff was a young boy. He was liable to mess everything up. That would come back and bite Roy. On the other hand, Garnett was a vet. Roy knew that he'll do the job right because that's what he did.

****

It's been weeks and Roy was still waiting to hear some tragic news about Marquita. He knew Garnett was going to get it done, but the anticipation was messing with him. Garnett assured him that bout time the next time they got up that it'll be handled.

Shamera had became Roy's main squeeze, but he was still dealing with other women though. They weren't living together, he had enough of that. She stayed over when he wanted her to. The thing Roy liked most about her besides her being a thorough chick was that she didn't complain. She didn't care who else he was dealing with. She wasn't money hungry, all she wanted was him. That made him really dig her. On top of the fact that she cooked and cleaned every time she came over. When Daniel found out about them, she started doing spiteful stuff like when it was his days with his daughter all of a sudden, they were out somewhere. She ended up putting him on child support, so he took her to court for joint custody. That way she had to let him see his daughter.

For a couple of months Roy haven't been able to sleep. The only time he was able to get some good sleep was when he had some liquor in his system. He started having dreams of his father. They brought back old suppressed feelings.

He got up early in the morning ready to go about his day. He was supposed to meet with Greg later on. He got up, got dressed and went about his day. It was a nice sunny day. Days like this in the hood anything was liable to happen. Roy went straight to the shop. Dame came through to re-up, and to give him the latest on the block. The only bad thing he said was that the detectives had picked one of their workers up and was asking him about dude who got killed that was trying to trap down the street. Of course, he didn't tell them anything because he didn't know anything. Also, he let him know that a Maxima with some white boys wearing suites kept riding through the block.

****

Roy got a call from Greg around seven. It was just getting dark. He was in his Grey tinted up Buick Lacrosse, one of the cars he be getting low in. Greg's manz got out of the Black Yukon Denali. Roy could see Greg sitting in his truck through his rearview mirror. Usually, he collected himself and punked Roy in the process but for whatever reason he didn't this time.

As soon as dude got in and got comfortable Garnett put the burner to his head and shot him three times. At the same time Roy jumped out of the car and started shooting at Greg. The first shot hit him in the shoulder. He put the truck in reverse and started backing out. Two more hit him in the chest. Roy was walking him down as he rapidly fired. While backing out Greg spent the truck around and drove off. Roy ran back to his car and sped off. Garnett had already kicked the other dude out onto the street.

CHAPTER 32

Greg's manz died. An officer was dead. The city was flaming hot. Roy moved from the house he was living in. Greg didn't say anything about who did the shooting. The news reported that the officers were ambushed, and that they were looking for two unidentified suspects.

Greg was shot in the chest and shoulder. He had crashed a few blocks away from the scene. Even though they said that they didn't have any suspects Roy wasn't taking any chances. He stopped going to Camden all together. He was running everything through someone else. Greg didn't get him jammed up. Roy knew that he wanted some kind of revenge. He wanted to hold court in the streets.

Months went by without Roy really getting any sleep. No matter how low he got he still felt as though he had to sleep with one eye open. He knew the Doom Squad had something up their sleeves. With everything that was going on he still kept in touch with Shon, going to go see him and taking his family up to Southern State Prison.

Roy decided to take a trip to Puerto Rico to go see his family and get away from the pressure. He arrived in Puerto Rico at night, checked into his hotel and took it down. It was the best sleep he had gotten in months. In the morning he woke up and ate breakfast.

He had been to Puerto Rico a few times when he was younger. Once when his dad was alive and a few more times with his grand mom, so he kind of knew his family there. His first day there he didn't visit any family members. He just wanted to clear his head. Being around people he didn't know gave him a sense of peace. He went shopping and pushed up on some chicks. He felt good just doing basic stuff. Stuff that if he was back home that he would have considered wack or boring.

The next day he left the resort and went into the hood of San Juan where one of his aunts lived. As he got out of the car it seemed like all eyes were on him. He knocked on his Aunt Chistina's door, no one answered. He could hear people in there talking loud in Spanish. He knocked again, this time a lot louder. A young girl answered the door with a stomach that looked like she was about due.

"What's good Veranica?"

"Roy, oh my god."

They gave each other a big hug. It's been years since they seen each other. Veronica was a little girl then, now she was seventeen and pregnant.

"Boy or a girl," Roy asked rubbing her stomach?

"It's a boy," she responded.

"If dude not good to you just let me know," Roy said as they walked in the house.

"Roy Roy," two of his little cousins ran up on him speaking Spanish. Roy understood everything they were saying, but his Spanish was chopped up.

His Aunt Christina came out of the kitchen wiping her hands. "Oh Roy, who you come here with," she asked hugging him?

"I'm here by myself."

Roy felt the love while at his aunt's house. She told him that he could stay there. He agreed even though the house seemed packed already. He just felt good being amongst his loved ones. When his cousin Behe first came in he didn't see Roy. Roy yoked him up.

"Yo, what the fuck man," he said in a deep accent before Roy threw him to the ground. He had the angry man face on until he seen who it was, then he got excited. Roy helped him up and they embraced each other. "Dam, you strong as hell to be so skinny."

"This that grown man strength," Roy said flexing his bicep.

"How long you going to be around?"

207

"Another day or two."

"Come out with me out tonight, I'ma get you some Island pussy," Behe said smiling.

****

They pulled up to the club in Behe's Red Camaro. He was getting money, during the whole ride he was telling Roy about it. When they got in the club the mommies were on them.

"Umm, who ya friend Behe," one mommy asked?

She was looking good. Roy would have settled for her, but Behe kept it moving after telling her that Roy was his cousin.

"She a around the way whore. You could get her anytime. I'ma get you some model type pussy tonight."

"I hope she thick like that one," Roy said looking around at everybody who was checking him out.

Behe walked through the crowd. As people spoke, he spoke back. They went upstairs and into the VIP section. Behe went over to a table that was full of people and started shaking hands. He introduced Roy. One of his dudes was sitting with his arms wrapped around two beautiful women. They were kissing each side of his face. He turned and French kissed one then turned to the other and French kissed her.

"Diego."

"Behe ma man," Behe and Diego slapped hands then Diego picked up his glass and started drinking.

"Diego, this is my cousin Roy from the states. Roy this my manz Diego."

Roy and Diego shook hands. "Diego made all the other chicks get up except the two that was on his left and right. "Have a seat," he told Roy and Behe. What do you drink Roy?"

"Rosè."

"Rosè it is then." Diego made a hand gesture to his manz and dude went to go get them a bottle.

"Behe told me some good things about you."

"I guest that's a good thing," Roy said.

Diego's manz came through with the bottle of Rosè. The chick that was next to Roy rubbing on his manz through his pants took the bottle and started pouring him and the other fellas their drinks. They sat there and politicked for hours. Diego was a cool dude. On the way to the club Behe had told Roy a little about him. One of the things he let him know was that Diego was a major connect.

After all the laughs cooled down Diego made the chick that was sitting between him and Roy get up so they could really talk.

"So, my friend, I hear you get money in the states. I got everything you need for the best prices, and I can get it to you."

Roy took another sip of his champagne before asking, "what kind of prices are you talking about?"

"I'll give them to you for 15,000. I'm basically bringing them to you."

Roy began nodding his head. "Yeah, you're right. I'm going to let you know."

Roy left the club with this beautiful thick Puerto Rican chick attached to him. They went to one of Behe's cribs. Roy was tipsy, but he planned on busting her ass. He was determined. Just the look of her turned him on. The mommy started kissing on him, he lifted her dress up and started playing with her pussy. She was dripping wet. He pulled out his manz and let his pants drop. They hit the couch and she began sliding up and down on his pole like a Magic City stripper.

"Oh Pappi," she said as she held him tight around his neck. She whined and moaned while she bounced up and down on his dick. She tensed up and started shaking, coming all over him. Roy could feel her coming, her juices dripping on his balls and legs as she continued riding him. After he bust off, she got on her knees and started slurping him. He leaned back while she went to work. Once she got it up, she bent over, and he started hitting it from the back. She grabbed his ankles. He was hitting it hard as she moaned all type of Spanish words, but she never let Roy's ankles go. It took about twenty minutes for Roy to get his second nut. He bust and they laid on the couch.

"That's what I'm talking about fam, you was beating that thing up. I got the whole thing on video," Behe said as he came off the stairs. Him and the chick that was with him was on the stairs watching and recording the whole thing.

"You on some freak shit. Ya'll was watching us the whole time.?"

"Hell yeah, that was like watching a porno. I'm about to go put on a performance of ma own. I'll send the video to ya phone."

O girl took Behe by the hand and led the way upstairs. Roy spent another day there. The day he was leaving his family took him to the airport and wished him farewell.

****

While in the air Roy had his phone on airplane mode, so he wasn't getting any of the calls or text messages. When the plane landed, he took it off of airplane mode and they came pouring in. All of them were talking about the same thing. That his club had been burnt down. Instead of going home he went straight to the club. There he met his club manager and a couple other employees. They all stood outside of the burnt building.

"I was trying to get in touch with you," Archie the club manager said. "The fire department said that somebody set the fire. They tried to burn everybody in there. It was chaos. People getting trampled, trying to get out."

Roy thought about who could have done something like this. "Ma insurance a take care of it," Roy said with confidence. The club money was just extra. It was nothing compared to what he was making in the streets.

Roy was riding through the city that he hasn't been to in months. He figured things had died down a little, but Camden was the hood. The things he was going through was just his story. It was always a lot going on out there. He rode through one set that vice was raiding. They had dudes out there on their knees with their hands behind their heads. Roy was trying to see the vice dude's faces to see if Greg or any of his boys were amongst them.

Roy hadn't drove his Bentley since the killing of Greg's partner. That car was known for being his. He had planed on selling it, but Sam kept asking him to push it, so he let him.

Roy was riding out East Camden near a construction site. A cop was directing traffic. He was in the middle of the intersection moving his arms back and forth for cars to come and go. When Roy got closer, he realized that the cop directing traffic was Greg. He leaned back in his seat hoping Greg wouldn't see him. He rode by then sat up. He couldn't help but to laugh as he watched Greg fad away in his rearview mirror.

Greg was put on traffic control because his story didn't add up to the internal affairs investigation. A cop had been killed and he was there, and they didn't have any suspects in custody. That on top of the complaints they had gotten over the years about him had got him demoted and put back in a uniform.

CHAPTER 33

Roy went to see his grandmom who he haven't seen in over a month. She was happy to see him, and he was happy to see her. She could never imagine the things he was going through in life. People like her knew that a lot of killings and crime took place in the hood, but they didn't know over what, or how it happened, or even the mind state of the dudes that did these devilish acts because like Roy, dudes only showed their grandmoms their good side. To her Roy would always be her baby.

"Hey baby, where have you been," his grandmom asked after he gave her a hug?

"I been chilling. I went to Puerto Rico to see some of the family."

"Why didn't you tell me you were going. How were they?"

"Everyone was doing good. They asked about you. Aunt Christina's daughter is pregnant. I just popped up on them. I went on a little vacation and decided to stop by."

"That was nice. You hungry?"

"Si, tengo humbre," Roy spoke in Spanish.

His grandmom had something delicious in the pot. She fixed him a plate and sat down to talk to him while he ate.

"How has Tierra been lately?"

"She's good, getting big. Her mom put me on child support."

"You must had really hurt that woman, Roy. A hurt woman will do whatever to try to get you to feel what she feels."

"It's to the point that she don't even talk to me."

"What did you do?"

"It's a long story, I wouldn't even know where to start."

"What about that other girl?"

"You talking about Marquita, she was no good. You know my club got burnt down, right?"

"I'm starting to worry about you Roy. You been going through a lot. Even though you don't tell me about it, I can see it on your face. Do you have anything you want to talk to me about?"

"Nah grandmom, I'm good," Roy said smiling. The last thing he wanted to do was worry her.

"You are just like your dad."

"It's ironic you brought him up because I been having dreams about him lately."

"I still have dreams about him too baby. He might be trying to tell you something."

"What do you think he trying to tell me?"

"I don't know. Maybe to not make the same mistakes he did."

Roy left his grandmom's house feeling good and full. Seeing her was always time well spent. The conversations they had about basic things relieved him of some stress. When he pulled off, he noticed a cop car behind him. He didn't think much of it, but when he turned the cop turned too. First thing that came to mind was Greg, he knew that Greg was a regular now. The cop put on his sirens. Roy pulled over. It was a lot of people out on a busy street so Roy doubted that if it was Greg that he would try something. Looking through his rearview mirror he was relieved to see that it wasn't Greg. The cop got out of car and walked up to Roy's car.

"May I help you officer," Roy asked?

"Yes, you may. Could you step out of the car Mr. Mckinnie?"

Roy was kind of stunned that he knew his name. It was a red flag, but he complied. Two other patrol cars pulled up to the scene for back up.

"You're wanted for questioning for the murder of Siddiq Samuels."

"I don't even know who that is," Roy said looking confused.

They didn't cuff him, but they did put him in the back of a cop car, then took him to the police station. They put him in a room and a homicide detective came in with a folder in hand.

"How are you doing Mr. Mckinnie? I got a few questions for you."

The homicide detective fired away question after question. Where were you August fourth? Did you know Siddiq Samuels etc.... They held Roy for about an hour, then let him go. Roy didn't know, but the dude who got killed on Atlantic friends, brothers, and cousins had told the detectives that it was because they was selling drugs out there. They had mentioned Roy's name and told them that he was a big time drug dealer. After a little background check they finally decided to pick Roy up for questioning.

Roy left the police station wondering how they even came to question him about that murder. He walked to the transportation center and caught a hack back to his car.

CHAPTER 34

Shon was a year and a half into his bid. He only had a 7 with 85%, meaning he would do five years and nine months. For a body that was nothing. He walked around with his head up high. His visits was coming every week, money stayed on his books and he stayed in touch with the hood. He was thorough, plus dudes who he was locked up with knew that he got money so that came with a certain status.

Shon and three other dudes were at the table eating mess when another dude from Camden came on the tier.

"He from the hood right there," Melo said.

Shon and the other dudes turned around to see who Melo was talking about.

"Oh, that's ma manz," A.Z. said. He stood up and called Trev's name then waved him over to come eat with them. Trev walked over with is tray in hand.

"What's good bro," Trev said.

Him and A.Z. shook hands and embraced. A.Z. introduced him to the rest of the dudes and they took a seat. Trev had caught a new coke charge, violated parole and got sent right back down state. He had just came on the tier so dudes hit him off with cosmetics and food to make sure he was good. Even Shon contributed. He didn't know him, but he seemed alright. They politicked with him. Regular beat downs, where dudes talk about their street tales, who mashed who, certain beefs or other things that went on. Shon never brought up his manz to nobody in conversations. He wasn't one of them dudes who lived off of the names of others.

A few weeks of being on the tier and Trev got comfortable and loose. The true him started to come out. He was one of them loudmouth dudes who talked too much. Not the type of dudes Shon like to deal with. He was always in the yard telling his war stories, lying about how much money he was getting and the chicks he was mashing. Most dudes in prison lived through their past and the stories they got from others.

"What Ron out there doing," AZ asked Trev?

"Ron out there doing him. He driving a 760 BMW. That thing nice, but his rims ugly. He mess with this chick, I forgot her name. Uhmmm Trisha, that's her name."

"I remember Trisha. She used to live near East Middle, right?"

"Yeah, that's her," Trev said.

"That bitch is a whore. What made him wife that?"

"I don't know, but ever since she been messing with him, she fell back."

It's true that some dudes in prison are worse than females when it come s to gossiping.

****

Shon had went to visit. His baby mom had brought the kids to come see him. He had three kids, two boys and a girl. The girl was only two years old, so he was holding her on his lap. Trev came strolling into the visiting hall like he was that dude for sure. Shon seen him and laughed on the inside. He knew that he was getting a visit because for the last couple of days he kept bringing it up, but Shon wasn't beat for what he was talking. He went out to visit every weekend.

Every time Shon was in visit, he always looked over at the visitors coming in. Every once in a while, he caught one of the chicks he used to be smashing coming to see someone he was locked up with, kissing them with the same mouth she used to suck him off with.

About five minutes after Trev came in the visiting hall, Shon saw Marquita come through the visiting side. She was the last person he was expecting to see. He wondered who she was coming to see, it was a lot of dudes waiting for their visits and a few was from Camden. Roy had told him about how she crossed him, but he never got the play by play on what happened the night he caught them bodies. All he had to go off of was the newspapers and rumors like everybody else.

Marquita checked in with the C.O. and her and Trev greeted each other with a hug and kiss. Shon's boys were running around playing and his baby mom was trying to collect them. Shon told them to sit down and stop playing around and they listened. Trev and Marquita sat on the opposite side of the visit hall from Shon, but he kept an eye on them. Marquita didn't notice him until visits were over and Trev sat near him and a couple of other dudes from Camden. When she seen Shon, she had got goose bumps all over. She was hoping that he didn't remember her.

As soon as Shon got to the tier, he tried to call Roy, but he didn't answer. He didn't get in touch with him until that night.

"What's good with you," Roy asked after pushing five so the lady could send the call through?

"Nothing much, what's up with you?"

"I'm chilling, it's hectic out here, but you ain't missing much."

"I hate when people tell me that bullshit. I'm missing everything," Shon said. "I went on visit today though. Do you know some dude name Trev?"

"Nah, why?"

"Because he in here on the tier with me and guess who came to see him?" Without giving Roy a chance to say anything he answered his own question for him. "Marquita."

"Yeah," Roy said. Then it dawned on him. Dude he bodied that night said something about Marquita setting everything up through his manz Trev who she was messing with. He started trying to remember what the dude who got away that night looked like. He couldn't, still he asked Shon. "What he look like?"

"Little brown skin, short, slim with waves in his hair."

Roy didn't have a vivid image in his head from dude that night, but short and brown skin sounded like him.

"Where is he from?"

"He be on Utah."

"Yeah, that's him," Roy said. "He was one of them dudes who she got to run in my house that night. Do she be coming up there on the regular?"

"He haven't been on the tier long. That was his first time getting a visit."

They kept talking until Roy's fifteen minutes was up. Once they hung up Roy knew that he had to put Garnett on Marquita's movements.

In Shon's eyes Trev was an enemy now, so he fell back from him. He stopped listening to his stories and laughing at his clown ways. Every time he came around

Shon spent off. He kept conversations short and tried to avoid them all together with him. Trev started to feel the vibe, but he didn't know why. He just thought that Shon was on some stressing stuff. One day about six of them was outside telling their stories, AZ had the stage when Trev walked up.

"I don't know where dude was from, but he pulled up in an all white Jag like he was Puff or somebody. Watch, chain out, picky ring sitting nice on some pimp shit. He walked right by us like he was like that. We out there looking at each other trying to see if anybody knew him. Nobody knew him. Make it so bad he left his car running. I told ma young boy hop in his car. He came running out the store all goofy like he was about to hawk it down. He pulled out his phone trying to make a call. I pulled out the burner on him and took everything. That's how we started beefing with dudes from 28th."

After AZ got finish telling his story Trev jumped in, taking the stage, trying to top AZ's story as if it was a competition. As if whoever had the best story was the more thorough one. Shon wasn't beat to hear anything he had to say. He was about to ease off until he heard his manz name.

"Ya'll know Roy that got the Bentley? Me and ma manz ran in his crib." As soon as he said that everybody got quiet and started looking at one another with raised eyebrows. Everybody except Trev knew that Shon was

Roy's manz. Even the dudes who didn't know him from the streets that been on the tier with him for a minute. When they looked at Shon he was smirking. He knew Trev was about to set himself up.

"Yeah, he a bitch, word up, he was begging for his life. I had the burner to him like." He had his hands like he had a gun in it, doing the motions while he was explaining the robbery. "He had the bitch in there too. I was smacking the shit out of her. She was bad, I wanted to hit, but you know I had to let them know I meant business."

Trev was lying trying to make his story sound as gangsta as he could. It took him about ten minutes to tell the whole thing. Shon just sat there listening.

"Word up, I came off with like three hundred thousand."

"You sure that was you? I heard he bodied two dudes that night. In fact, he got locked up for it, didn't he," Shon asked Melo acting like he was trying to get him to co-sign what he was saying?

"Nah, what happened was, we had got into a shoot out and both of ma dudes got hit. They died, but I got away. You know how it is. I'm still going to get at him for that though."

Trev mistake was running his mouth without knowing who he was around. Even though they were fly he didn't know them dudes or who they dealt with on the streets.

Everybody was quiet. They messed with Shon more than Trev. AZ was the only one who really knew Trev from the streets. Shon acted like he agreed with Trev. As soon as Trev turned his head the other way Shon stole off on him with a right. He didn't put him down. Trev staggered a little and Shon kept hooking off on him. Trev had his head down holding on, then he started kicking up. He regrouped kind of fast from the punch and him and Shon started going at it. Dudes that were there had broke it up before the C.O.'s came.

"You weak, you stole me and ain't put me down. I'ma see you on the streets. I'm telling you, buy ya tux," Trev yelled as two dudes from Camden held him back.

Not long after he found out why he got punched in the face. Later that day dudes let them lock in the room and fight. The agreement was as long as no one got stabbed or used anything else besides their fist. Dudes watched out for the C.O.'s and they got it in. Shon won, they both came out with bumps and brushes, but the winner was obvious. Trev wasn't a punk. He just couldn't beat Shon. Even though they agreed not to take it any further while they were locked up, they both knew that it wasn't over. That they were more than likely going to see each other on the streets. Camden was too small for them not too, so they preserved their beef for then.

CHAPTER 35

"Pass that bottle," Garnett said taking the bottle from Game.

"Yo bro, you know I love you right? I'll do anything for you. Never forget that. Anybody you need me to get at just point them out."

"I'm good bro, you drunk," Game said.

"You know them Vice dudes that got hit up not too long ago?"

"Yeah, why?"

"That was ma work," Garnett bragged. "I bodied him for Roy. He was apart of the Doom squad. They were extorting him so he paid me to pop his top."

"Why you telling me?"

"Because you ma manz."

"When you do stuff like that you don't tell nobody, ya manz, ya mom, her mom, nobody. Then you talking around these bitches."

Game called O girl a bitch while she was right there next to him. They was in one of their spots chilling getting drunk. Garnett was letting the liquor get the best of him.

"They're good, they're more thorough than a lot of dudes."

"That ain't the point. I don't care if they was apart of the Doom squad, they had badges. That ain't something you want to take lightly. Ya manz Roy ain't built like that. I don't' care how much money he got. I'm telling you. I know a bitch when I see one, rather they got on a skirt or jeans. I'll get at him if I was you, just to protect myself. Don't let that shit come back and bite you in the ass."

Garnett knew Game was talking some Real stuff. He sat quiet taking it all in. Not long after Game had stop talking Garnett received a call from Roy.

"Yo," he answered.

"I got a scoop on that chick."

"I'm tipsy right now, I'ma talk to you tomorrow about that." He gave no indication to Game that it was Roy on the other end of that phone.

The next day Garnett and Roy got up. Roy put him on how Marquita was going to see Trev every week in Southern State Prison. He really wanted her dead. She tried to get at him and was moving around like everything was sweet. They couldn't find her nowhere in the hood so once Roy put Garnett on her movement he went to the prison on visiting day and plotted on her.

He sat in the car like he was waiting for someone. He knew he was out of pocket, but in his military mind he was going to do whatever it took to accomplish his mission. He watched the entrance and the parking lot as the visitors got out of their cars and entered the prison. He peeped Marquita strutting, unaware that she was being watched. He didn't see what car she got out of but now that he knew she was in there all he had to do was wait a couple of hours for visits to end.

He went to the store and got something to eat. Garnett peeped her coming back out when visits were over. She jumped in an old Tan Taurus. Garnett was thinking how Roy would have definitely had her driving something better than that. He tailed her from a distance. She had a heavy foot. He lost her in traffic. He was upset with himself but at least he knew what she was driving now.

That night he went hunting for that tan Taurus. He even rode through some enemy territories. Of course, he was in an unfamiliar tinted up car. His gun sat on his lap. He spotted the car outside of Sunshine Grocery store, but no one was in it. He went around the block, came back and pulled over on Haddon Ave, down from the set so dudes couldn't see him. The car was faced in the opposite direction for his getaway.

Haddon Ave was a main strip. Even at night it was lit up, but Garnett didn't care about that. A cop car rode through the Ave a second time. Garnett got low until it passed. Once he saw Marquita come out, he hurried up and got out of the car leaving it running for his return. He jogged across the street, his gun tucked in his sleeve by his side and the other hand on his stomach. He was trying to catch her before she got in her car, but it was parked right outside of the store. In the mist of him trying to hunt down his prey somebody started shooting at him. Somebody from Parkside had peeped him and thought that he was trying to creep. Garnett started shooting at Marquita while getting low between cars. The shots were hitting her car, she was screaming and running, cars were trying to get out of the way. Garnett seen the dudes that was shooting at him dip into an alleyway. Marquita jumped in her wheels and sped off. Garnett emptied the clip shooting at her car. He hit the car up, the window busted out, but he didn't know if she was hit.

Garnett told Roy how he had her, but dudes messed everything up. He explained how everything went down and reassured him that things were still going to get handled. Garnett was more frustrated than Roy. Roy wasn't sweating it as much. He knew Marquita would eventually get what was coming to her.

Roy was playing the hood heavy again. He still had people moving out for him, so his movement was to a minimum. He didn't know if he was bugging or what, but he felt like he was seeing the same cars following him. He always rode around before going to his destination, but he knew he was being followed. That made him cautious about how he was doing things.

On top of him being a little paranoid them nightmares he was having were becoming more and more vivid. It was to the point he could see his dad and hear his voice. The night his pop died he kissed Roy and tucked him in good night. That night Roy went to sleep thinking about school. School excited him when he was young. Instead of waking up for school he woke up to loud noise. He didn't know what it was, but his ears were ringing. He got out of bed and seen his dad struggling with another man. His ears were still ringing, he stood there watching, then dude shot his dad. He seen his father fall to the ground. Right in front of him the two dudes shot his father to death. The same man who shot his father walked up to Roy and put the gun to his head. That's when Roy woke up in a cold sweat. He sat up real fast.

"Are you alright," Shamera asked?

Roy didn't respond, he took a couple of deep breaths, then got out of bed and went to the bathroom. He took a piss, washed his hands and threw some water on his face, then looked at himself in the mirror. His subconscious had revealed something to him. He couldn't believe it. He finally realized where he remembered RamPage from. He was the dude that had the gun to his face the night his father got killed. The same dude he seen his father tussling with.

Everything was clear to Roy now. RamPage was one of the dudes who killed his dad. It was 3:38am, but Roy was up. He couldn't go back to sleep. He didn't even try. His mind was going a hundred miles an hour. Now he knew the reason why whenever him and RamPage was around each other there was an awkward vibe. He could never place his finger on it. The only other person he used to feel like that around was Greg and he knew why he felt like that around him. He despised him.

RamPage was a natural enemy. All Roy could think about was how he would get revenge. He wondered if RamPage even knew that he was that little boy from that night. When Roy's father died Roy cried for weeks. Them feelings from when he was seven had came back. The anger, the bitterness, the hurt, he remembered how vulnerable he felt. This was personal, something Roy wanted to do with his own hands. That could be the only way he got the full satisfaction of revenge.

****

The Whole day Roy couldn't stop thinking about it. He tried to go about his day, but everywhere he went someone would ask him what was wrong because it looked like he had a lot on his mind. At the shop he was present, but his mind wasn't there. His mind was busy coming up with ways to make RamPage pay for what he did. He had to come see Roy to re-up soon.

CHAPTER 36

Sam was shinning in Roy's Bentley. He was extra cool with his shades on, hat to the back and arm hanging out the window, flossing his watch. He had Roy's car for months and started telling people that it was his.

Friday morning Sam had just come into Camden to go to Work at the shop. As soon as he got on Kaighn Ave a cop had pulled him over. The car was legal, fully insured and Sam had his license, so he wasn't worried about anything. The cop didn't get out of the car right away. Sam assumed he was still running his plates. Sam knew the proper procedure, he been around long enough. He was trying to figure out why he had gotten pulled over. He knew being a young black man in a Bentley was enough for most cops to want to see his credentials. The police officer finally got out.

"License and registration please."

Sam had everything waiting already. He handed it to him as soon as he asked for them. The cop examined it right there.

"Cut your car off and hold tight.," the officer said and walked back to his car. It took about five minutes before the cop came back.

"Step out of the car please."

"What's the problem officer?"

"Step out of the car," the officer commanded.

"Shhh." Sam shook his head and got out of the car. *It's always something,* he thought to himself.

"Put your hands on the car and spread your legs."

Sam did what he was told, and the officer began searching him. Patting his left arm then his right arm.

"Where ya boy Roy at," he asked?

"What," Sam questioned. Either he didn't hear him clearly or he was questioning what he had heard.

"I asked you where ya boy Roy at," the cop said again checking around his waist? He wasn't searching him how the cops search people when they get pulled over. He was searching him how they searched dudes when they got ran down on for selling drugs on blocks.

"I don't know who you talking about," Sam responded irritated.

"Why you lying? This his car." The cop was now searching his legs and digging in his boot.

"This is my car," Sam said.

"Stop fucking lying."

Sam shook his head in disbelief. He couldn't believe that this cop was coming at him like he was. Then out of nowhere he got punched in the face from the back. His head went to the right. It almost put him out because it was unexpected. He grabbed the cop trying to hold him, but the cop was hitting him with all type of hooks and ups. Sam held on though. Another police cruiser pulled up to the scene. Sam didn't see him because his back was turned. He began swinging back. While they were fighting the cops gun dropped and they ended up on the ground wrestling.

"He got my gun," the cop on the ground yelled. They both were getting off of the ground. Sam seen the other cop with his gun pointed at him. He didn't know what to do. He was like a deer caught in headlights. "Shoot him, he got my gun," the cop said again.

Clearly, he didn't have his gun because the other officer seen the gun on the ground near Sam's feet. Afraid for his life Sam took off running. When he did the officer who he was wrestling with quickly grabbed his gun, got up and shot Sam three times in the back. Then ran over there and jumped on him and handcuffed him.

Sam survived but had gotten a slew of charges. He was in ICU when Roy tried to go up there, but no visitors were allowed in. While at the hospital he was approached by Greg.

"You like my work? That was supposed to be ya punk ass. I got you though, it aint over," Greg said with a smile on his face. He was the uniform officer who Sam was fighting with.

When Roy heard about Sam's situation it didn't occur to him that it could be Greg's work, but now he seen what it was hitting for. Greg was on some BS. That same night he had gotten a call from some girl telling him that Jeff was locked up and needed him to come bail him out. Roy agreed to get him out the next day. One thing Roy knew was that you don't leave dudes like Jeff in jail, no matter the situation. He was too valuable and knew too much.

The next day Roy and the chick got together and went to the ABC bondmen and paid for Jeff's bail. The chick stuck around for her man to get out. Roy didn't, he had stuff to do. When Jeff got out, he called Roy and they got up that night.

"Good looking bro," Jeff said finally getting a chance to thank Roy for getting him out. "I called my supposed to be manz and them dudes kept giving me the run around. I'm done with them."

"You mean to tell me you out here doing all this dirt and you don't have bail money."

Roy always looked out for Jeff, but Jeff never could stay focused. He was a thorough dude but surrounded himself with bums.

"You know how it is bro. One minute I'm up, next minute I'm down. This just happen to be one of them times when I didn't have it."

"You gotta stop playing and get ya shit together. You got a connect, I'm right here so you can't use that as an excuse. I'm not going to push anything on you though. If you really want to get money it'll show."

"You right you right. I been really thinking about that boxing thing. It's getting real whack out here."

"I'm behind you with that too. Whenever you ready, just let me know."

Jeff was feeling like he was really ready to give boxing his all, even though he wasn't in shape. Talking to Roy made him feel bad about having potential and not using it. The next day he called old head who had given him his number in Las Vegas at the gym and they set everything up for him to fly out there in a couple weeks.

CHAPTER 37

Roy had got the call that he had been waiting for from RamPage. He hadn't thought everything through, but he knew he was going to make him feel it. He called Jeff because he knew he was going to need help.

RamPage got in the car and started talking. Roy played along like everything was everything. He gave Roy the money he owed him, and they went to one of Roy's spots. The house was an abandonminium, but Roy owned it. He didn't get around to fixing it up because he had so much other stuff going on. He just been using it as one of his stash spots.

RamPage was surprised that he trusted him enough to take him to one of his spots. He took mental notes incase he ever needed to double back. Roy went to the kitchen cabin and grabbed a bag. RamPage was behind him. Jeff came up behind him and put the gun to his head.

"What the fuck," RamPage said turning around. Jeff stood there mean mugging like he was waiting for him to make a move. "What's this about," RamPage asked turning back to look at Roy who was now holding his own gun?

"What it look like? Have a seat, we have to talk about some things."

RamPage looked around and didn't see any chairs. Jeff kicked a crate his way. He looked down at it, then reluctantly sat down.

"Tie him up," Roy commanded. Jeff gave Roy his gun and started wrapping RamPage up with duct tape.

"You know Tuco is going to have ya head for whatever you do, right?"

"Get off of Tuco's dick, he ain't going to know nothing."

When Jeff got done Roy stood in front of him and looked down at him and asked, "You ever think about the people you killed?"

"Why would I? More than likely I killed them so I wouldn't have to see or hear them no more."

Roy looked at him with an evil eye. "You know when we first met, I felt like I knew you from somewhere or like you did something to me before. Did you get that feeling?"

"Man, I never did anything to you."

"Oh yes you did. My father was Antonio. I watched you murder him when I was seven. I remember you holding the gun to my head. Your biggest mistake was that you didn't pull that trigger. Now I got the gun to ya head," Roy said pointing the gun to his face. "How does it feel?"

"I don't know what you talking about," RamPage lied. He knew exactly what Roy was talking about.

Jeff was in awe of what he was hearing. He didn't know anything about this. To him this was some movie stuff. Revenge for a father's death. That was something he only seen on Chinese karate flicks.

"You could leave now if you want. I just needed you to help me tie him up," Roy told Jeff while putting on his gloves. RamPage started sweating, but he stayed gangsta.

"I'm good, this is going to be entertaining," Jeff said.

Roy grabbed the blow torch out of the cabinet. For the first time RamPage showed that he was scared.

"Come on man, what you plan on doing with that? I'll do whatever, I'll give you whatever, just please."

"You broke, what could you possibly give me. Tape his mouth up and help me take him downstairs."

Jeff did what he was told, and they took him downstairs. RamPage was squirming making noise the whole way. Down the basement they had a chair they placed him on.

"Tie him to the chair," Roy said chuckling. Now RamPage was crying. "I only have one of these," Roy said holding up the face shield that the welders used to protect their eyes.

Jeff went to the steps to watch what he thought was entertainment. Roy didn't waste any time. He pulled down the shield and lit the torch. The blue flames had it looking like they were on a construction site. As Roy walked towards him, RamPage started going crazy trying to get out of them restraints.

Roy started with his feet. As soon as the flames hit him, it melted his sneakers, skin, and meat. Roy moved the torch between both feet. RamPage fell over in the chair, but Roy kept going. He started trying melt bone. RamPage was crying so hard that no noise came out. He was in agony.

Jeff was looking making faces like he could feel RamPage's pain. He covered his nose from the burnt human flesh he was smelling. Roy wasn't having any mercy on him. He stopped when he seen skeleton feet. That's when Roy turned the torch off, lifted his mask up and took a look at his work. To see RamPage suffering made him feel good.

"What are you going to do with him now," Jeff asked walking up to Roy still covering his nose?

"I'm going to body him. I just want him to suffer for a couple of hours. Shit, I suffered for years when he killed ma pop."

"You think they can smell him out there?"

Roy looked at his watch and answered, "nah it's late, shouldn't nobody be out."

"Let's go out front so I can smoke this dutch," Jeff said. They went outside and sat on the steps while Jeff smoked. No one was outside on that block besides them. "Yo bro, do you ever really think about the life you live?"

"I'll be lying to you if I say I didn't. This ain't no way to live. That's why I be telling you, go do that boxing thing while you still young and can."

"What about you? I know you got enough money that you can leave. You can disappear and go anywhere you want."

"You right, sometimes I think about that." Roy got quiet as he went into deep thought. "You ever heard of the story with the Monkey that was trying to get the apple out of the box?"

"Nah, what about it?"

"The box had a hole in it the size of the monkey's fist, but when he grabbed the apple his hand swelled up so he couldn't get it back out. The dumb monkey kept trying different ways to get the apple out, but he couldn't. This went on for hours to the point the monkey just wanted his hand back. He started jumping around going crazy. He felt trapped. He didn't realize that all he had to do was let go of the apple and he'll have his hand back."

"What's the point," Jeff asked without a hint of where he was going with it?

"Let me get some of that Roy said."

Jeff gave him an uncertain look and he passed him the dutch. Roy took the dutch and held it like a cigarette.

"Ma point is that it's hard to let go. Unlike the monkey I know that if I just let go and leave all this shit behind that I'll be good. It's just hard."

They sat there talking for a while longer, then went back inside. When they got downstairs RamPage was passed out. They didn't know if he was dead or not. To make sure he was Roy put the mask back on, lit the torch, knelt down and melted his face. RamPage's body started shaking, then it stopped.

They put him in a plastic bag, took him outside and put him in the car. Roy drove to a quiet street, popped the truck, poured gasoline on him and throughout the car and lit it on fire. They walked around the corner and got into a Tahoe.

****

Roy sent Jeff to Las Vegas with $30,000. He let him know if he needed anything to let him know and he'll western union it. He told him to just box, that's all he wanted Jeff to worry about.

CHAPTER 38

J.B. was going in the store on 9th street right behind Virtual hospital. A dude ran in there on him. As soon as J.B. seen him, he tried to pull out, but dude had already started hitting him up.

Garnett had got a call about what happened. He stopped by where the fellas were at to get the full scoop.

"It was somebody from Parkside," Game said.

"It's back on," Garnett asked?

"It was never off. Word is we shot the Ave up." That's bullshit though, I asked everybody, ain't nobody do it."

Garnett didn't admit to it, but he knew it was because of what happened the night he was trying to get at Marquita.

CLICK CLACK CLACK. Game had put the drum on the Dracco and cocked it back.

"I'm riding, hold up," Garnett said. He was trying to get rid of his guilt with some revenge. It didn't work though. He didn't get any action because no one was out. Their manz who was in one of the other cars shot someone on Empire, but they wasn't sure if he was a hood dudes or a civilian who lived out there.

****

Roy had started trying to push Garnett to get rid of Marquita. He had paid him a lot of money and patience wasn't going to make it happen, so he asked Garnett what was the hold up. Garnett went back to the prison and squatted on her again.

Trev was in the gym playing basketball when he was called out for a visit. He wasn't expecting one. He rushed back to his tier to take a shower, put on his visit clothes and went to visit not knowing who had came to see him.

"Hey baby," Marquita said as she hugged him around his neck. They kissed and Trev's dick got hard.

Marquita could feel it growing as she pressed against him. "Sorry I haven't been on my bike how I'm supposed to be. I been under a lot of pressure lately. I think Roy had somebody try to do something to me."

"Why you think that?"

"Somebody was shooting at me. Why else would someone want to shoot me?"

"You grimy as hell. I know you done did something to somebody you forgot about."

They both found that funny.

****

Back on the tier Shon and Trev had a cold war going on. They gave each other mean looks, but that was the farthest it went. The tension was building and dealing with the same dudes didn't help. Certain dudes were running back and forth on some he said stuff. That caused Shon to fall back from everybody. He wasn't with the extra stuff. He could wait until they got to the streets.

CHAPTER 38

Roy had gotten the call he was anticipating. Tuco called asking about the death of RamPage.

"When that happened," he asked faking like he was shocked and didn't know?

"They said he was found over Philly burnt up."

"Dam, over Philly."

Tuco never expected that Roy had anything to do with it. He knew RamPage stayed in something. The funeral was basic, just family and friends. Roy didn't attend, but Tuco did. Afterwards him and Roy got together.

"What happened to the Bentley," Tuco asked seeing Roy Driving the Tahoe?

"Ma manz got shot up in it."

"Dam, you alright out here. Ain't nobody putting pressure on you, are they? Told you I'll send ma boys down here if you need me to. I'll sick my boys back there on whoever and they'll attack." Tuco was referring to the two shooters that was in the car riding behind them. They rode to Camden with him.

Roy didn't have a doubt of what his shooters a do. He seen the work of the last two dudes he sent.

"I ain't got them type of problems. I know how to make ma money work for me. I'm like Tony Montana in this city," Roy said not only making himself laugh but also bringing a smile to Tuco's face.

"I guess I'm Sosa then," Tuco said with a little sly grin. Where was RamPage getting money at?"

"He used to be downtown on 6th and Royden."

"You know any of them dudes?"

"Nah, I only dealt with him on the strength of you. I don't just deal with anybody. That's how dudes get swept up in them indictments."

Tuco nodded in agreement.

Later that day Tuco rode through 6st and Royden with his henchmen. He sat in the back of the Benz as his driver pulled up on a dude that was chilling on a step with a chick. He was a Spanish guy with braids. His skinny jeans were sagging and even though he was grown with a clean shaven face he looked like he didn't care about much. It wasn't hard to tell that he was a hustler. He stood up when the car stopped in front of them.

Tuco rolled the tinted window down so he could be seen. "Young soldier, can I talk to you for a minute?"

Dude hesitated, took another pull of the dutch then gave it to the chick that was chilling with him. He diddy bopped over to the car as Tuco got out.

"I'm RamPage's uncle," Tuco said giving dude a handshake. "Did you know him?"

"I heard about you and seen you in some pictures. RamPage was my manz. We were like brothers."

"What's your name?"

"Cho." Dude answered.

"Did you hear anything about what happened to him? I know the streets has to be saying something."

"If I would have heard anything they would be dead already," dude said with conviction.

Tuco could tell that he meant what he said. He also ruled him out as somebody who could have done it. He knew usually when dudes get tortured it was from somebody they knew who they was comfortable enough around to let their guard down.

"The last time we were together he told me that he was going to re-up. I remember before he told me something about his connect that I don't even think his connect knew. I forgot dude name he was getting coke from, but he told me that back in the day he had slumped his pop. I guess dude didn't know, but to me whoever dude is, he amongst the suspects. That was the last time I saw him though."

Tuco knew who the connect was. He just didn't want to accept that Roy would do something like that, knowing that he was his family. The whole while Cho was talking Tuco was trying to find holes in his story that pointed in another direction. There was none. Roy wasn't only suspect to Cho, he was now suspect to Tuco as well.

In the car Tuco thought about RamPage and when he was younger. His sister said that his face was melted to the point she had to identify him by his tattoos. Thoughts of how his family was crying at the funeral. Then he started thinking about the money him and Roy was making together. The two hundred thousand he had coming his way from Roy. Too much to lose. Roy was Tuco's only source in the city, but Tuco's family came first. Another source could always be found. Dudes were always looking for connects.

****

"Oh, I almost forgot," Amy said digging around in her little briefcase. "Here is the information you asked me for. He works for the police department," she said handing Roy the papers."

"I know, he's just an old friend I need to get in touch with."

Roy got out of bed and put his boxers on.

"Let's take a shower together," Amy said. She got out of the bed and began pulling on him. If it was left up to Roy, he wasn't going to take a shower. He was going to leave and go about his day how he usually did after he got some pussy.

Amy convinced him though. Her little petite white ass looked like it belonged on the cover of playboy. Whoever her husband was he wasn't doing his job, it seemed like at least once a week she was calling Roy to get hit.

Roy picked her up and pinned her against the shower wall. She liked to kiss so he tongued her down. He turned her around and started hitting it from the back. She was making all type of noises. He started choking her out. He would squeeze her neck hard for about fifteen seconds, then let go, giving her some air. He knew exactly how she liked it. She was the one that turned him on to the s and m stuff.

CHAPTER 39

Roy and two of his dudes were waiting for their mark to pull up. It didn't take long. Greg arrived right on time. As soon as he did Roy pulled out of his parking spot and pulled right behind his car. Greg had got out of his car and went to the passenger side to help his little daughter out. He didn't pay the car that pulled behind him any mind. The suburbs was a safe haven, so he thought. Out there he wasn't just a law abiding citizen, he was the law, a hero. That was the image he portrayed.

Greg helped his daughter out of the car. He put her pink bookbag around his shoulder and held her hand as they walked towards their house. His daughter couldn't have been no more than eight. The whole time Roy was observing him. This was the other side of Greg. Now he was seeing a man that had everything to lose. He just thought that no one could get one up on him.

BEEP BEEP!

Greg and his daughter kept walking. She was looking up at him and he was looking down on her like they were talking. Roy started beeping his horn again. BEEP BEEP BEEP! Greg and his daughter kept walking. Greg turned around looking at the car with three dudes in it. He was looking hard trying to see if he knew anybody in there.

Roy got out of the car smiling. His energy was different from any other time when he seen Greg. "So, this is where Greg live at huh," Roy said still rubbing his palms together as he nodded his head? He was basically letting Greg know that he had the drop on him. He wasn't even looking at Greg, he was looking past him at his house. Greg's daughter rang the doorbell, and a lady answered the door. She was looking at Greg trying to see who he was talking to. She took the little girl in the house. Roy made sure he had gotten a good look at her. She went in and shut the door. Roy seen her peeking through the blinds.

"What the fuck you are doing coming to my house?"

"Watch ya mouth," Roy said. "Have some respect." Roy was giving Greg what he usually gave him.

Greg wasn't expecting to hear those words come out of his mouth. He thought he had him punked out. Roy gave him a stern look letting him know he meant what he said. Even though he was looking up at him he was standing tall.

"You look like you comfortable out here, real safe like. You know what this mean, right? This mean that you could be touched," Roy said without letting him answer.

"Is that some kind of a threat," Greg asked?

"I ain't here to make any threats, I'm here to let you know that I'm tired of playing games. It's one up. Ya manz dead and you almost killed me and ma manz. Let's leave it like that so nobody loses."

Greg didn't like that he showed up to his house, nor did he like how he was coming at him. To top it off Roy had brought two other dudes with him who now knew where he rested. Roy wanted to show him if he tried anything else that it's more people who know where he lived that'll get at him.

Greg knew that Roy was on some bullshit. He really wasn't giving him an option. Either you go along with it or I'ma bring it to your doorsteps where ya wife and kids live, is what Greg had got as the underlining message. Greg looked in the car at the two dudes that was watching him the whole time.

"You got it, we're going to leave it as that. I think that'll be best for the both of us," Greg said and put his hand out for a handshake.

"Ain't no need to shake on it, just don't violate," Roy said as he left Greg's hand there and got in his car.

Greg wanted to slap the shit out of him with that same hand. In his mind Roy wasn't built how he was acting. It was hurting his soul to let him get away with threatening him like that. He stood there and watched the car as it pulled off hoping his wife didn't see him get dissed. He fake waved at the car, then turned around towards his house where he seen the blinds snap back. He knew somebody in there was being nosey.

Roy didn't shake his hand because he didn't believe that he'll hold up his end of the agreement. He just had got caught slipping and didn't want any smoke where they were at. Roy knew to stay on point, and he had something for Greg if he tried anything.

He dropped his comrades off and went to go meet Tuco. Tuco had invited him to go out. They met up in front of the shop. Roy didn't like for people to know where he lived.

"I thought you went back up top," Roy said. He was in the back seat behind Tuco. It was four of them in the car. Tuco's two dudes wasn't doing any talking. "You might as well buy a house out here if you going to be down here on the regular."

"I might end up doing that. Who was ya father Roy?"

Roy paused for a minute as he got nervous. He knew this had something to do with RamPage. He looked at the other two dudes who didn't pay him any mind. They held a serious emotionless face. He processed all of this quickly as he tried to give a smooth response.

"His name was Antonio," Roy responded. When he said his father's name dude who was in the back seat with him looked at him for a second as if he knew Roy's father and wanted to see if they looked a like or something. Then he turned back around.

Persuasive Contracts | TyeMease

"I know a couple Antonios. What was his last name?"

"Hernandez," Roy responded.

Tuco was trying to figure if he knew him. "When did he die?"

Roy didn't want to be ignorant because he respected Tuco, but he wasn't feeling that he kept on with the questions about his dad. He knew something was up because he never said anything about his father being dead so how did he know.

"He got killed back in the day. I don't remember what year."

The thought of his death made him think about how he just got his revenge after all these years. He wanted to smile, but the same thought made him nervous as he remembered that his victim was Tuco's nephew. Things became uncomfortable, and he got tensed, but he still tried to play it off like he didn't mind talking about it.

"I need you to give me what you got of that money before I head home," Tuco said.

"I could get it for you right now. It's not far from here."

"Alright, where to?"

255

Roy told him and he pulled out his phone and started texting while still talking. When they pulled up to the house Roy got out and knocked on the door. While he was knocking, he looked back at the car. They all were looking at him, probably wondering why he was knocking instead of going straight in.

A short brown skin chick answered the door and Roy walked in. As soon as he shut the door, he pulled out his phone not saying anything to the chick as she just looked at him wondering what was wrong.

"Where ya'll at," Roy asked?

"We're right around the corner."

"Tear that shit up. They strapped too so make sure ya'll don't let up."

"We got it."

Roy ended his call and looked out the window from the living from. The blinds were open, and the house was lit up because of the lights, but they couldn't see him from where he was standing.

"What's wrong Roy," the chick asked?

Candy was a stripper chick Roy was hitting when he wanted. He didn't really care about her that's why he took them there. If things ain't go right and something was to happen to her he wouldn't lose any sleep.

"Nothing, come here." Roy took her hand, and they went upstairs to her bedroom. Roy looked out of the window in time to see the Blue Camry pull up alongside of Tuco's car. The long nose of a gun came out the window and shots rang out. Another dude had gotten out of the car and ran around and started hitting the car up from the back.

The shooting went on for what seemed like minutes. Candy held on to Roy tight with her head buried in his chest while he stared out the window. Then the car sped off. Tuco stubbled out of his car with so many holes in his shirt that it looked like a Jamaican ting top. He fell, then got back up and limped in the street. Roy came from the back of the house and ran up on him.

"You ain't think I knew you knew. You tried to vet me, but I was on point. It was nice doing business with you."

Roy put the gun to his head and finished him off. BOOM! Tuco's head jerked back and a piece from the back of his head flew across the street.

CHAPTER 40

"What's good Shon?"

"What's good bro?"

Melo spoke to Shon who was on the phone talking to the mother of his kids. Trev had walked by Shon too, but they didn't pay each other any mind. Trev had been stressing for the past two months. Marquita haven't been coming to see him and he was messed up on the money tip. He was in the day room in Melo's face telling him about it, but Melo was standing there with his arms folded looking like he wasn't beat. Instead of getting the hint Trev kept on rambling.

"She ain't come up again bro. I keep calling home. I hear her pick up, but she won't accept ma calls man. I just wrote her a black out letter, word up." Trev sounded like he was about to cry.

"Fuck that bitch man, you don't got life," Melo said. He knew Marquita and knew how she got around. Melo knew how women started power tripping when the ball was in their court. Being as though this wasn't his first bid, he had been through it before with a couple of chicks, but he didn't act like Trev. What Trev was doing was embarrassing not only to himself but for Melo as well. Dudes from out of town was close by, listening, looking at him whine. Every dude locked up go through it with their ladies and family, but it's about how you handle it that measured your thoroughness.

"You don't understand, she got all my money and I'm in here fucked up."

Melo seen a tear fall down his cheek. He looked around and seen that other dudes wanted to laugh, but was holding it in. Melo grabbed Trev by both shoulders and shook him real hard about five times then said, "snap out of it you bitch ass mothafucka." Then he grabbed the front of Trev's shirt, cocked his hand all the way back and slap the shit out of Trev. SLAP! His hand went to the other side of him. He brought it back with the back hand leading, then once more with the front hand. SLAP SLAP!

Trev hit the floor holding his face, looking up at Melo like he was crazy. Trev ain't never been bitched smacked before. He was so shocked he couldn't even react. He was trying to confide in Melo, he didn't think he would be slapped for it. Melo felt like he had embarrassed them though.

"Fuck out of ma face crying like a bitch. I don't want to hear that shit. If a bitch get me for ma money I'ma off her. I ain't going to cry about it. I suggest you do the same."

Shon was on the phone laughing, telling his kid's mother what had just happened. Melo came out of the dayroom and walked by Shon with a smirk on his face. "That's how you treat dudes who act like bitches."

****

Roy's plane landed in San Juan Puerto Rico. As he left the airport the tropical air played tricks on his allergies. *I don't know why I don't come here more often,* he thought to himself. Thoughts of buying a spot out there came to mind. That way he wouldn't have to check in at a hotel, or with his family when he went to visit. If everything went his way on this trip, he'll be making Puerto Rico his second home. Since he killed his connect, he had to replace him. Good thing he met Diego when he did.

"Yo," Behe said answering his phone.

"What's good cousin."

"What's up cuz, when the next time you coming out here?"

"I'm out here now, in front of your house."

Behe opened the front door with the phone still to his ear. He had on shorts, no shirt and his bedroom slippers. He signaled for Roy to get out of his car and come in. Roy came in and seen two Puerto Rican chicks walking around half naked. He couldn't help but to admire them. He liked the way Behe lived his life.

"You gotta stop popping up like this."

"That's what I do. I ain't come out here to chill though. I'm trying to make a move with Diego."

"Alright, you just on time because I was heading over there soon. Let me get dressed."

Behe went upstairs threw some clothes on and came back down in ten minutes. They left leaving to the two chicks behind.

"You just going to leave them there?"

"Why wouldn't I, they're ma girls," Behe said like it was nothing. "They know better than to take anything. They already getting a free ride."

Roy nodded his head in approval. He leaned back in the butter soft seats of Behe's BMW and within a half an hour they were pulling up to the gate of this estate. Behe pressed a button, and he was buzzed in. They rode up the driveway pass a few dudes with machine guns. A Rose Royce, Bentley, and a May Bach was a few of the cars that costed a quarter of a mill or better lined up along the driveway. Roy was impressed. Diego was really on another level.

Behe had called Diego and had let them know that they were on their way, so he was out front ready to greet Roy with open arms.

"I knew it was only a matter of time," Diego said shaking Roy's hands. He invited him in, and they toured the house. Diego was introducing him to his staff along the way. *This is how your money is supposed to treat you* Roy thought to himself while Diego was telling him how he got everything built from the ground up. Roy knew it was one thing to have money, but to really do something with it was another thing. He was inspired and vowed to step his game up.

"So, you came to see about that?"

"I thought it was about time I took you up on your offer."

"What do you need?

"I'll take thirty five of them off of your hands," Roy said looking at Diego to see his facial expression. *I hope he ain't think I came out here to waste time,* Roy thought. Diego wasn't impressed though, he wanted to unload more than that.

"How long will it take you to finish them?"

"Probably close to three weeks."

"That's good. Alright I'll front you another thirty five and we'll make this a monthly affair. How do you like that?"

Roy brooded for a few seconds. He knew messing with Diego that he would have to step is flow up because the pressure was on. He was going to have to expand. He was up for the challenge though. "I can handle that," Roy agreed, and they started talking numbers.

****

"What's good Shon?"

Shon heard the voice, but he had to turn around and see for sure if it was who he thought it was. Shon looked Trev in his eyes and nodded giving his tacit what's up, then turned back around to get his food.

They haven't spoken in months. Trev knew they were enemies, but the more Marquita shitted on him the more he wanted to patch things up with Shon. A chick that wasn't riding with him wasn't worth riding over. She haven't written or visited him in over six months. She had got him for all of his money, including what he robbed Roy for. He was stressing to the point he started getting skinny. Stress, on top of that he didn't really have money on his books to buy canteen. He had dark circles under his eyes, and he needed a haircut.

"I know we haven't been on good terms, but can I talk to you," Trev asked walking behind Shon?

"About what?"

"I got something that you and ya manz could use."

"What's that," Shon asked as he sat down?

Trev took a seat next to him. "I know ya manz is trying to get at Marquita. I can hand her to him. I know where she's staying."

"Where at?"

"1047 Pierce Street."

"And why are you telling me this?"

"To tell you the truth, it's because she shitted on me."

"So basically, you hurt because ya chick not playing her part so now you want her bodied and you want my peoples to do your dirty work for you?"

"Nah bro, I ain't on it like that."

"You going to have to handle that when you touch. You go home soon, don't you?"

"Yeah," Trev answered disappointed in Shon's answer. Shon never looked at him while he ate his food. He listened and was giving him the cold shoulder. Trev felt played, but he knew he was reaching. He hurried up and ate and got up from the table.

Shon had got the address out of him, but he wasn't going to agree with him. He didn't trust him like that.

****

"What's good bro? How you holding up in there," Roy said answering the phone?

"I'm good. What's up with you though? I been trying to get in touch with you for the last couple of days. I was starting to get worried."

"I was in PR trying to get everything right. The shit I been through is the type of stuff you only read in them one of them TyeMease novels. I can't wait for you to touch though. What you got about two and a half left?"

"Yeah, something like that. I should be in the halfway house soon. Did you get my letter?"

"I didn't get a chance to check my mail. I just took it out of the box and threw it on the table."

"When you go home check it out. It's something in there you might can use."

"Alright, I'm a come see you this weekend. I gotta send you these shots of these PR chicks too. They get loose out there. I'm about to cop a spot out there."

When Roy got home, he read the letter. Shon wrote like a two page front and back letter and added the address that Trev gave him at the end. That night Roy got up with Garnett and gave him the address. It wasn't a doubt in his mind if he still wanted her dead or not. He had already paid for it to get done.

Roy had been without coke going on two weeks now. He had let Dame cop something from someone else while he took some time for himself. This was like the first time since he started hustling that he didn't have coke. In his mind real hustlers didn't take breaks. Even when vacationing somewhere their business was still fully functional without them there.

****

Shon came in the visiting hall shining. Other dude's chicks were checking him out. His waves were spinning, and his weight was up. Shon had told his lady to fall back because Roy was coming up. Once Shon spotted him, he went over where he was.

"Okay, I see you getting your weight up," Roy said as they shook hands and embraced each other like brothers.

"Can't leave out the same way I came in. Plus, I gotta stay strong in case I gotta beat the breaks off of one of these dudes."

They sat there talking. Roy was updating him on what was going on in the real world, how he had got a different connect and was about to make Puerto Rico his second home.

"That's dude I had told you about right there," Shon said as Trev walked in the visiting hall.

"Yeah, he look like he could be the dude from that night. I have to get a closer look so I can remember his face." Then Roy seen Marquita come in. Her and Trev shared a hug and a kiss.

"Look at this shit here," Roy said.

Shon turned around and seen them kissing. "His tender dick ass was just bitching about how she wasn't playing her part. He a sucka. You know Melo?"

"Yeah, I know him."

"He smacked him up for crying on the phone over her."

"I'll be back," Roy said and got right up.

"Don't start nothing bro," Shon said as Roy walked over to them.

When Marquita saw Roy the hair on her back and arms stood up. She wanted to run and scream like Jason was coming. Instead of doing all that she sat there with the little sad puppy face. Trev was shocked also, but he tried not to show it.

"I just wanted to let ya'll know that ya'll look good together," Roy said smiling. They should bury ya'll together because I'ma kill both of ya'll. You won't get away next time," he said then patted Marquita on the shoulder and walked away.

"You ain't going to do shit," Trev said getting loud. The other visitors who were close by was looking at him like he was crazy. Trev had the angry man face on like he wanted sauce. All that time he spent stressing because Marquita wasn't visiting him didn't mean anything. She was there now, and he was back simping. "You should go stay with your family on the out skirts or something," Trev advised Marquita.

"Why you say that," she nervously asked?

"Because I think he had someone go in my cell and steal my stuff. Some of my mail was missing, the ones with your address," Trev lied. He couldn't admit that he tried to get her bodied out of spite. Marquita looked at Trev disappointed, but it was nothing she could do. "I'm sorry baby, just lay low until I touch. I'll handle them dudes. That way you won't have to worry."

Roy was looking over at them smirking while talking to Shon. The smiles and delight that Trev and Marquita were enjoying before Roy came over was now gone. After visit Roy watched Marquita jump into a Tan Taurus that was about ten years old. He found it funny how she went from sugar to shit.

CHAPTER 41

"I ain't bring anything with me today. I didn't want to tell you on the phone, but I'm kind of in transition," Roy told his lawyer. His lawyer's mouth dropped. Roy could tell that he was really looking forward to getting high tonight. "I apologize for the disappointment." Roy knew that he was not only disappointing him, but he was also disappointing everyone who was there.

"It's alright," Mr. Gilbert said fixing his face. "I Have another friend I can get it from. He's Muslim so he doesn't come to stuff like this, which mean I have to go get it. He's real big business, but play it real low key. No fancy cars or anything. I might could bring you two guys together if you would like."

"I'm alright right now. I'm just waiting on a shipment," Roy said.

Roy walked around chatting with other people. Every time he attended these gatherings he was dressed appropriately. He didn't want to be the odd ball out around all the suits and ties, so he wore an Armani suit.

"Mr. Mckinnie," Roy heard a voice say. He turned around and seen Nancy looking good. She was the prosecutor chick he had gotten fly with. He heard that she was a beast in the court room, but every time they ran into one another at these gatherings it was a flirty type of vibe between them.

She threw her arms around him like she was excited to see him. He hugged her around her lower back, she kicked her left leg up. She had on a black suit jacket and skirt with some heels. Standard office wear for her. She held Roy as they chatted. Roy seen other people looking in amazement. They never really seen her hugged up with anyone before. She was married but her husband didn't know that when she came to the gatherings that she dibbled in a little nose candy. Nancy had suggested they take a ride, so they did.

****

Game had just pulled into the parking lot when he seen Roy get out of a Grey BMW with a white woman. He looked at the plates on the car and could tell that they were some type of officer of the law tags. That didn't sit right with him.

"Hold on, don't get out," he told the chick he was with. She already had one foot out the door when he told her that. Being from the hood she didn't ask any questions. She knew something was wrong. Game waited until Roy and Nancy went in the store then pulled off.

****

"I can't believe this shit, got me moving out of my house because his punk ass let somebody rob his cell." Marquita was packing her things and talking to herself. She couldn't believe that she had seen Roy. If she hadn't Trev wouldn't have told her what he told her. She wouldn't be moving out, but Roy confirmed that what Trev had said was true. She took his threats serious because she knew that it was nothing for him to give the word and something would get done.

****

"Come on baby, I got you this time," Garnett said as he cocked his gun. He kept seeing the curtains open up and Marquita a look out. He wanted to wait until she came out, but he was running out of patience. He got out of the car and went to the side of the house and peeked in the window. He saw her bring a bag downstairs. That's when his phone rang loud. He quickly grabbed it and answered it. He squatted down and started talking.

Marquita came to the side of the window looking to see who was out there. She had thought she heard something. After not seeing anything, she went back to doing what she was doing.

When she had came to the window Garnett knew she was there because of her shadow. When she left, he started talking.

"Yo," Garnett whispered into his phone.

"I told you ya manz was suspect."

"This ain't a good time. I'm in the process of a mission right now."

"I hope it don't have anything to do with ya boy. If so abort, for real. I need to talk to you. He is working with them people, I got proof. Where you at?"

Game was his manz, if he said he had something then he must really got something. Garnett aborted his mission. "Alright, meet me at B.U.'s house."

When Game pulled up Garnett hopped in the passenger seat. "Now what you talking about," he asked?

"I'ma show you," Game said. He pulled into the parking lot where they could clearly see the car Roy came in. Twenty minutes later Roy and Nancy came out of the restaurant.

"There they go right there," Game said.

"Alright he with a white girl. He probably tricking," Garnett said trying to make a joke of it. He was squinting his eyes trying to see exactly who she was. As he zoomed in, she started looking more and more familiar. Once he realized who she was he frowned in disbelief. "Yo, that's that prosecutor bitch that was trying to give me all that time. What, he been trying to set me up so they could bury me?"

"I hate to say it, but I told you so. Something in ma soul just told me that he wasn't right."

"I'm ready to knock his head off," Garnett said pulling out his gun and taking it off safety.

Nancy was trying to pull out of the parking spot when Game pulled up behind her cutting her off.

"Aye, what's your problem," Nancy yelled looking back at the car.

Roy turned around and saw Game and Garnett getting out of the car. "What the hell is these dudes doing," Roy said in a low voice, but Nancy heard him?

"Do you know these guys," she asked?

Roy didn't answer, he didn't have a chance to. Game and Garnett was already on both sides of the car with their guns pointed. Game had his gun pointed at Roy when he opened his door. Roy held his hands up.

"Get ya bitch ass out the car."

Garnett opened the driver side door holding his gun to Nancy's face.

"I'm a Camden County District Attorney," Nancy stated as if Garnett was supposed to respect that.

"Bitch shut up, I know who you are. You don't remember me, do you," Garnett asked bending down showing her his face? She was shocked to see the man she had been trying to prosecute, but who had went on the run. "Don't act shocked now. This how it feel to be facing thirty year in prison."

"Garnett, this me, what's going on?"

Nancy was easing out of the car. In between her and the armrest was her gun. In one sly motion she grabbed it, took it out the holster and wrapped her finger around the trigger. Garnett couldn't see the gun because her hand was a little behind her. As she stood up Game seen the gun from his side and yelled, "she got a gun!"

On hearing that she tried to lift it up to take aim at Garnett, but she wasn't fast enough. Garnett shot her twice in the face. She hit the ground and he hit her two more times.

"Oh shit," Roy said.

"Put that pussy in the truck," Garnett said.

It's like that Garnett," Roy asked petrified. He couldn't believe his manz was trying trunk him.

"Hurry the fuck up," Game told Roy. Roy was slowly easing in the trunk while pleading to Garnett about going in there.

Bang! Garnett punched him in the face dropping him in the trunk. One leg was still hanging out. Game pushed it in and slammed the trunk shut, then they spent off.

Roy was scared to death in that trunk. Even when he opened his eyes, he couldn't see a thing. He could hear Game and Garnett talking but couldn't make out what they were saying over the music. They had been riding for so long that Roy began losing feeling in his right leg. He had to take a shit bad and kept passing gas. His stomach was going crazy. Every time something was wrong his stomach a start talking to him.

Roy felt the car come to a halt, the doors opened and closed. He wasn't really a believer in God, but he figured he'll give praying a shot. He closed his eyes and put his palms together.

"Dear lord, I know I did a lot of wrong in my life, but I promise if you deliver me out of this situation alive, I'll change my ways. I'll leave everything and square up. I promise God, just one last chance, I'll do the right thing."

Roy was begging God for another chance when the trunk opened. When Roy opened his eyes, he thought he was in heaven until his eyes adjusted to the light and he seen Game standing over top of him mean mugging. *This can't be heaven, I know he not making it,* Roy thought to himself.

"Dam you stink, what you shitted on yaself? Come on out of here," Game said frowning up his face from the smell of Roy's constant passing gas. As Roy was able to stand some feeling came back to his leg. He looked up and seen Garnett standing with his arms folded. Game was posted next to him. Roy looked around but was unable to tell where they were. It was just a dirt lot with grass and trees around.

"What type of cop shit you on," Garnett asked?

"I ain't on no cop shit, you got the game fucked up."

"Well explain why you was with that prosecutor chick that's trying to give me all that time."

"I was about to go hit."

"I ain't going with that," Game said. "You expect us to believe you fucking a prosecutor?"

Roy looked at Game like he was stupid. "This is what I do, I'm connected. I got lawyers, prosecutor, cops, judges, and politicians on smash. That's how it really goes. If I would have known that she was the prosecutor on your case, I could of worked my magic for you."

Neither Garnett nor Game was believing anything he was saying. Having prosecutors and judges on the hip was beyond their comprehension. They were street dudes. To them if you were caught talking with the D.A. you were snitching.

"You done killed the bitch now though. I'm saying, I might could still make something happen for you," Roy said.

"What you think I'm stupid? I ain't going back to jail," Garnett said and pulled out his gun.

Roy got scared as Garnett got aggressive. "Hold up, this me Garnett. I'll never tell on you." He seen that Garnett had that look in his eyes.

"Look I got seventy bricks in the air right now. They should be landing any moment, ya'll could have them. I'll pack up and leave the city. Forget everything, seventy bricks, think about it," Roy said looking at both of them seeing If they would bite. Game and Garnett were looking at each other then back at Roy.

****

Meanwhile the feds were on Diego's every move. He had been under investigation for the past eighteen months. He led them to Roy, and they added Roy to their investigation. They followed the shipment from Puerto Rico until it landed in Philly. Roy's dudes were

277

unloading and loading the bricks into their van when the Feds swarmed them. Simultaneously they had another squad kicking in Roy's house door looking for him.

****

"When are you going to get the coke?"

Roy was relieved to see that Garnett was interested. That was a sign of hope. "I was supposed to be there now. I could have everything to you tonight, guaranteed."

BOOM! Roy stood there for a second then fell face first onto the ground. Garnett looked over at Game who had just shot Roy in the side of the head.

"Why you kill em? We was about to get seventy bricks out of him."

"Man, we would have been in prison facing the death penalty messing with him. He would of told everything he knew. I'm not chancing it."

Persuasive Contracts | TyeMease